rules for life

rules for life

DARLENE RYAN

ORCA BOOK PUBLISHERS

National Library of Canada Cataloguing in Publication Data:

Ryan, Darlene, 1958-
Rules for life / by Darlene Ryan.

ISBN 1-55143-350-8

I. Title.

PS8635.Y35R84 2004   jC813'.6   C2004-905222-5

Library of Congress Control Number: 2004112453

Summary: When her mother died two years earlier, Izzy thought the world would change
in some identifiable way, but it didn't even slow down. She has managed to get by using her
mother's endless "rules" as guidance, even making up some of her own as she goes along.

Orca Book Publishers gratefully acknowledges the support for its publishing programs
provided by the following agencies: the Government of Canada through the Department
of Canadian Heritage's Book Publishing Industry Development Program (BPIDP), the
Canada Council for the Arts, and the British Columbia Arts Council.

Cover design and typesetting by Lynn O'Rourke
Cover illustration by Kathy Boake

In Canada: **In the United States:**
Orca Book Publishers   Orca Book Publishers
Box 5626, Stn. B   PO Box 468
Victoria, BC   Custer, WA USA
V8R 6S4   98240-0468

08 07 06 05 • 6 5 4 3 2
Printed and bound in Canada

Acknowledgments

Special thanks to Lori Weber and Stacy Juba for reading an early draft of this book. Thank you as well to Sharon Wildwind for answering my questions about hospitals, Everett Runtz for letting me pick his brain about cars, and Ann Cavan for trying to teach me where to put the commas.

Thanks as well to Kevin Major, a wonderful writer and teacher.

And thank you to The New Brunswick Arts Board for support and encouragement.

For my mother and sister.

1

I knew my father had had sex the minute I walked into the kitchen. It wasn't as though he was smoking a cigarette and basking in the afterglow. It was subtler than that.

But I knew.

It was his hair. Dad is really particular about his hair. It's strawberry blond, like mine. He spends more money on shampoo and conditioner and gel than I ever would. I just wash mine and twist it up in the back. He goes to a stylist at a salon where you have to make an appointment two weeks in advance. I go to the walk-in place and take whoever has a free chair.

Dad wears his hair sort of long for someone who's forty. And the whole left side was flattened against his head, with a few pieces coming out at weird angles, like he'd slept on it funny. Which meant he'd slept somewhere else, because the first thing he would have done here when he got up was shower and fix his hair.

So I knew he'd had sex. Plus I could see the neck of his T-shirt in the vee of his sweater. It was inside out.

And backward.

I got my cereal out of the cupboard—two blobs of shredded wheat—boiled water in the microwave, poured it on my cereal and drained it off. My breakfast looked like a dish of soggy hay. It's what I've eaten every morning since I was four. My mother always made it. I ate it. When she wasn't here anymore, I made it.

A bowl of fiber to start the day was one of my mother's rules. She had a lot of rules, and if you asked her why about any of them, she'd smile and say, "Because I'm the Supreme Ruler of the Universe, that's why."

And I almost thought she was, until two years ago when she died and the universe didn't even slow down, not for a second. It just kept on going.

But I liked knowing my mother's rules, even the weird ones that I didn't really get. So I started writing them down—all that I could remember—in a little red notebook I kept on my dresser. I got up to fifty-three.

One of my mom's rules—it's **number eleven** on my list—is **Don't talk to Izzy in the morning.** Now it's not like I'm some kind of foul, nasty person when I first get up. It's just that I like to think about things and chew and not talk for a while. Shredded wheat takes lots of chewing, you know. And the more you chew, the bigger it gets.

So my dad didn't say anything to me. He sat at the end of the table with his smushed hair and his turned-around T-shirt and a big, goony grin on his face.

After half a dozen spoonfuls I glanced over at him, and his face flushed, as though he knew that I knew what he'd been doing. The thing is, we talk about everything. My friends think it's either so cool or deeply weird, but realistically, who else am I going to talk to? My mother is dead. Unless I want to hand out $3.99 a minute to the Psychic Seers Network we're not going to be doing a whole lot of talking. And my big brother Jason is not someone you talk to. He's usually someone you talk about.

So my dad and I have this deal. I can tell him anything, and he can tell me anything, and neither of us tells anybody else.

Dad cleared his throat a couple of times. It sounded like Spencer, my cat, trying to hack up a fur ball.

"I spent the night with Anne and I think I'm in love with her," he said. (My dad, not the cat.) He said the words so fast it took me a few seconds to sort them out into some kind of sense.

I looked at him again. Who was Anne?

"No. No, I don't think I love her. I know I do." He looked surprised by what he'd just said. "Truth is, Izzy, I liked Anne from the moment I met her. I always felt great around her. She's kind, she's gentle, she's smart. So we started spending all this time together, as friends. And I thought that was all it was going to be."

He got the dopey look again. I'd finally put a face to the name. Anne.

My dad is a consultant on a TV show where these two designers go around decorating rooms for people. It sounds boring, but the two guys are so funny and they bicker like an old married couple, so lots of people tune in who would probably never watch that kind of program. Anne had started working on the show at the beginning of the year.

Say the guys are decorating a bathroom and they decide to put the toilet paper in a basket. Anne was the one who went from store to store to find the best toilet-paper baskets and then dragged them back to the office. Another day she might be looking for old lava lamps or handmade quilts. I'd met her once or maybe twice. All I could remember was someone about my height with short, dark hair.

"I always felt happy when I knew I was going to see her," Dad said. "I felt…like a teenager again. And then one day I kissed her and I couldn't stop."

He couldn't seem to stop talking, either. I mean, I know in the abstract that my father has sex. He's a guy. He's good-looking. He's not that old. But I don't want to *know* he's doing it. I don't want any details. Just because we talk about every-thing doesn't mean he has to tell me everything. I don't want to start thinking about body parts and sweaty sheets.

So I nodded. I couldn't talk anyway. I had a mouthful of shredded wheat that wasn't getting any smaller no matter how much I chewed. **And if you can't say some-thing nice… (Rule #6.)**

"I'm going to ask Anne to marry me," Dad said.

I did a cartoon spit-take. Milk and strings of cereal sprayed everywhere. "Marry you?" I choked out. "You had sex with someone a few times and now you want to get married?"

His head snapped around and his smile disappeared. "Watch your tone, Izzy," he said softly.

I reached for a piece of paper towel to wipe my mouth and buy some time. "But why get married?" I asked in the reasonable, good-girl voice I use on teachers and authority figures. "Can't you just have a torrid affair?"

"I love Anne," he countered in his own reasonable voice. "I want to spend the rest of my life with her. And I want us to be a family."

"We already are a family."

"I mean a real family."

I leaned across the table and squeezed his arm. "You feel pretty real to me, Dad. Although you might have a point about Jason."

He shook his head, but he couldn't help grinning. Then his face got serious again and he stared at me so long I felt twitchy. "Don't you miss having a mother, Izzy?" he asked.

"I have a mother," I said. I knew where he was going with that question and I wasn't going to follow him. "Okay, we can't exactly go shopping, but I don't like shopping anyway." I smiled like it was no big deal to me.

"I love Anne."

"That doesn't mean you have to get married." I crumpled the paper towel and dropped it on the table. "C'mon, Dad. It took two tries with Mom to get it right. Face it. You aren't the home at six, minivan kind of guy."

"I've changed. Living with your mother changed me. Living without your mother changed me."

"But not into a totally different person." I almost pointed out that he'd stayed away all night and hadn't even called. "And maybe Anne likes things the way they are."

His coffee cup was empty, but he kept fooling with it, picking it up and setting it down. "What do you have against Anne? You don't even know her."

"Yeah, I don't know her. I've said maybe four words to her. And you're telling me you want to marry her." The last of my cereal was a wet blob in the bowl. It looked like something even a horse wouldn't eat. I pushed it to one side.

"Well, if that's the only problem, you can get to know her," Dad said. He got up and put his cup in the sink. "We'll all have dinner tonight." He smiled as though everything was fine again and ran his hands back through his hair. "I'm going to take a shower."

"Hey, maybe I have plans tonight," I called after him.

"You do. Be ready at six thirty."

I pulled the bottom of my sweatshirt up over my face, clapped both hands over my mouth and screamed. All you could hear was a faint, high-pitched sound that probably had all the dogs in the neighborhood howling.

I slumped back in the chair and tried to think of one of my mom's rules that might help. The only one that I could come up with was **Rule #26: If duct tape won't fix it, chocolate will.**

I had a feeling this was going to take a lot of chocolate.

2

"**M**rs. McKenzie, could I ask you a question that's sort of personal?" I asked. I adjusted the angle of the video camera so the old lady was in the center of the frame. I was working on my Communications project, a documentary on women at work over the last sixty years or so. *Then, Now and In between* was the working title.

It was a hoot interviewing women at the Seniors Center. I was expecting they'd mostly been teachers and nurses and secretaries. Already I'd met a professor, a pilot and an ecdysiast (a kind of stripper with big feather fans).

"You can ask me anything, dear," she said.

I tilted the camera up slightly on the tripod. Perfect.

"I don't mean for this," I said, gesturing at the camera. "It's just something I was … curious about."

"Go ahead. What is it?" she said.

"Why did you get married again? I mean after the first time."

"Which time do you mean?" she asked. "I was married three times altogether."

Three times? Okay, that probably shouldn't have surprised me. Mrs. McKenzie had already messed up my ideas—okay, my prejudices—about old people.

I mean, she looked the way you would expect someone's grandmother to look: fluffy gray hair, flowered dresses with buttons up the front and matching belts, sensible shoes. She made the most incredible chocolate chip cookies, plus oatmeal cookies with raisins and giant gingersnaps too big to dunk whole.

On the other hand, she loved the Rolling Stones.

You want to know what's truly weird? Watching someone who's about a hundred and six coming down a hallway toward you wearing headphones and wailing, "I can't get no satisfaction."

I remembered her question. Which time? "Well, um ... all of them, I guess," I said.

"Jimmy was my first love." She smiled. "We were only married two years when he died. A month later I found out I was in the family way."

Family way? Oh yeah, she meant pregnant.

"I didn't know enough to be scared," she went on. "I was so happy that part of Jimmy was going to live on."

"So what about ... number two" I asked, sliding into the chair next to the camera.

"Oh, when we met it was like something in a movie. I slipped on the ice and Richard caught me."

"You're kidding?"

She shook her head. "He said when I fell for him, he fell for me." She grinned at the joke. "Six months later he asked me to marry him."

"And you said yes," I said, folding my legs up under me.

"Actually, I said no."

"No? Why?"

"Well, my mother always said you should know a man through all four seasons before you marry him." She patted her gray curls. "I hadn't thought I would get married again, after Jimmy. But Richard was kind and strong and he adored the twins. I wanted them to have a family. And I knew we'd be happy."

"But they did have a family. They had you."

"It's not the same," she said, shaking her head. "I wanted them to have two parents."

"But maybe it's not what they wanted."

"They were as crazy about Richard as he was about them."

I wasn't crazy about Anne and I'd bet she wasn't crazy about me.

I hesitated, not sure if I should ask, and then I did. "Did you love him?"

That got me another smile. "I know it must sound kind of strange to you, dear," she said, "but I loved all three of my husbands. Every time I took my wedding vows I truly meant every word."

"So what about your third husband?" I asked, twisting in the hard chair. My right foot was going to sleep.

"Oh my," she touched her cheek and actually blushed. "Malcolm was the most incredibly handsome man I had ever seen. I decided on our first date that I was going to marry him." She gave me a smug little grin. "And I did."

"Mrs. McKenzie, you fox!" I pretended to be shocked, then grinned to show I was only kidding.

I stood up, shaking my leg to get the blood flowing again. "Thanks," I said. "Ready to start taping?"

"Any time," she said, giving her hair one last pat and crossing her ankles like a perfect lady. I was still trying to get the feeling back into my foot. Maybe I needed to start sitting like that.

I took one last fast look through the lens and opened my notebook to my list of questions. I asked Mrs. McKenzie the first one, but as she answered, my mind wandered back to what she'd said before. So my dad was getting married because he wanted to give me some kind of new family or because he was horny. Great. It didn't matter what the reason was. It wasn't going to work. He'd married my mother twice. I remember one time her saying he liked the idea of being married better than the real thing.

There was no way this would work. There had to be some way to stop it.

Rule #18: A good plan is better than a good excuse.

What I needed was a good plan.

3

I slid my arms around Rafe's neck and kissed the hollow spot on his neck just below his ear.

"Quit it," he said. "You're making me crazy." He stopped typing and pointed at the computer screen. "Look. That whole line makes no sense." He lowered his voice. "My dad is in the kitchen. And anyway, isn't it the sixteenth?" Rafe keeps better track of my periods than I do.

"You're the one who's making me crazy," I said, flinging myself melodramatically back across the sofa in the Kelly's family room. "My father stayed out all night last night and I was home at nine thirty."

Rafe made a face. "Gross. Don't talk to me about your father having sex. I don't want to think about anyone's father or mother doing it."

I folded my arms under my head. "Well I don't know about anyone else's parents, but my dad was doing it last night and now he wants to marry her."

That got Rafe's attention. He turned from the computer. "Your dad's getting married?"

"No!" I came up on my elbows. "I mean, he wants to ask her, but that doesn't mean it's going to happen."

"That's generally how it works, Izzy," he said.

"Not always."

Rafe came and sat on the edge of the sofa. He's your typical Nordic god—blond hair, green eyes, wide shoulders and tall, about six foot three. In a word, yummy. And we fit together perfectly because I'm five foot seven, which is kind of tall for a girl.

We met about six months after my mother died. I was making microwave popcorn in the *Informer* (the school newspaper) office. Next thing I know the room is full of smoke. Rafe comes tearing in with a fire extinguisher and blasts the microwave halfway across the room. Oh yeah, and pretty much destroys the mock-up of that week's edition.

You might say the sparks were there between us from the beginning.

"So what's the potential evil stepmother like?" he asked.

"That's the thing. I hardly even know her. How can my father marry someone I barely even know?" I flopped against the cushions again. "We're having dinner tonight."

"Does she have a name?"

"Her name's Anne. She started working on the show back in January," I said.

"You mean the blond with the big—" I shot him a warning look "—teeth?" he asked.

I shook my head. "You never see Anne on air."

"Maybe you'll like her."

"Yeah and maybe I'll spontaneously combust too."

"Oh, come on, Izzy. Give her a chance." Rafe gave me his best pretty-please smile. Easy for him. His parents have been together about a week less than forever.

"I never told you that my mom and dad were married twice, did I?" I said, sliding down so I was sitting on my tail-bone.

"What do you mean, 'twice'?" Rafe said.

"They were married and they had Jason. Then they got divorced. I think Jason was about two. Then a couple of years later they got married again and had me."

"But then they stayed married."

"Only because my mother was crazy about him. And she could do everything. So it didn't matter that he'd get caught up in some project and stay in his shop for two days, or that he didn't notice Jason had flushed someone's shoes down the toilet." I sat up. "See, husbands are like your dad. They have practical cars and sensible hair and they come home for supper. That's just not my dad."

"If your dad gets married, it could be great," Rafe said. "A whole new life."

Except I didn't want a new life, thank you very much. I liked the old one.

"Kiss me," I said. "I have to go home and get ready."

Rafe leaned forward and his mouth came down on mine and his tongue slid inside. For a second I couldn't breathe and it seemed as though I could hear the rush of hummingbird wings in my ears. And the thought flashed through my mind: Was that what Dad felt when he kissed Anne?

4

I stood in the bathroom, one leg hiked up on the sink, carefully pulling the razor up my left shin. Tricky work. The Lady Sophisticuts razor (cuts, get it?) was supposed to adjust to the contours of my curves. What it generally did was knick me somewhere. I'd been suckered by a catchy TV jingle again.

I thought about pitching the Sophisticuts and swiping my dad's razor. It was his fault I was doing this anyway. But **Rule #23** got in the way: **A woman should have her own razor and her own bank account.**

Somehow I managed to shave both legs without severing any major veins. Then I filled the tub with hot water and eucalyptus oil and soaked until I was totally pruned. Spencer wandered in while I was drying off. The eucalyptus made him sneeze. He swished his ginger tail at me and stalked off.

What to wear? Skinny blue skirt with the slit because if I'd gone to all the trouble to shave my legs, then they were going to show. Purple shirt because it was my favorite. The bracelet Rafe gave me for Christmas—a string of amber beads—because I always wore that.

Then I took down my wooden treasure box from the top of my dresser and sat on the bed with it. It was about a foot long, maybe eight or nine inches wide. Set into the wooden top was a teddy bear, sitting with his head tipped to one side. It took forty-three pieces of wood—six different kinds—just to make that bear.

My dad made the box when I was nine. It's what he does. He makes things out of wood—mostly furniture. It seems bizarre that anyone would pay hundreds or sometimes thousands of dollars for a chest or a bed, but they do. Of course a lot of the stuff he makes now is for the TV show.

I lifted the lid of my box and took out my mother's silver and amethyst bracelet. I fastened it on my arm above the beads and put the box back. **(Rule #20: Chocolate chip cookies and good jewelry go with everything.)** My mother might be dead, but she was still my mother. I knew that, even if my dad seemed to have forgotten.

I did the fast makeup thing and twisted my hair back into a low knot.

Ready. Now what? It was only five to six.

I wasn't good at waiting. I ended up at the computer trying to finish the script for my video. I got so into the words I didn't even hear Dad and Anne come in.

Suddenly, there they were. We kind of smiled at each other awkwardly because we had met before, but we didn't know each other. Anne had short, dark hair that curled all over her head. She was a couple of inches shorter than me and at least seven or eight years younger than Dad.

But what struck me was that she was nothing like my mother. My mother had shiny blond hair the color of corn silk. And even when she was mad at you, her eyes never stopped smiling. She was almost as tall as Dad, with long, long legs. He'd tease her and say he only fell in love with her because she had legs up to her neck.

"What are you working on?" Anne asked, gesturing at the computer.

I gave her the short version of my project.

"It would make a good history project, as well," she said.

"Yeah, I guess," I said, shutting down the computer.

"I have my dad's collection of 78s," she said. "Let me know if you need some music from that era."

Seventy-eights?

"Vinyl records," she explained, guessing from the "duh" look on my face that I didn't know what she was talking about. "Old ones. And I have a turntable to play them on."

"Um, thanks," I said. Great. Here she was being nice to me and I hadn't even decided yet if I wanted to like her.

I turned to my dad. "Is Jason meeting us here?" I asked.

"I left him three messages but I haven't heard from him."

My first thought was that I was going to kill Jason for leaving me to do this all by myself. That's what Jason did. He acted like a shit sometimes, and where did that leave me? Because he was three years older he'd gotten to be the selfish, rebellious one, and by the time I came along, all that was left in the box was nice.

And then for a second I wondered if he was out getting wrecked somewhere. Had he fallen off the wagon, off the straight and clean path he was on these days? That was mean of me. I wondered if I was ever going to stop thinking that way.

"Ready?" Dad asked.

"Sure," I said. I was a lot more ready than Anne, who looked queasy and uncomfortable.

We had dinner at a little Greek restaurant. Anne and Dad talked about the show and I talked about school and we were all very polite.

I was back in my jeans with my feet on the back of the couch and my head on the floor—I was hoping for inspiration to hit so I could finish my script—when Dad came in from taking Anne home. They'd dropped me off first.

"So, what do you think?" Dad asked, picking up the pile of mail from the table by the door and shuffling through it.

"I told you what I think already," I said.

"So tell me again."

"Okay. I don't see why you want to get married."

He looked up. "How can you feel that way now that you've gotten to know Anne?"

"The only thing I know about Anne is that she has a collection of old records and she doesn't like black olives."

He closed his eyes for a second and took a deep breath. "All I want is to be happy. I want us to be a real family again. Is that so bad?"

"Well, what have we been up to now, Dad?"

"You know what I mean," he said.

"I don't think I do," I said stiffly. "What's so wrong with our life?" I dropped my legs to the floor and sat up. "We always have birthday cake, and turkey at Thanksgiving. We have clean underwear and toilet paper and all the bills get paid on time. We're a family. You and Jason and me. Even Mom. She's still a part of this family even if she is dead. No one's in jail. No one's getting stoned on the street—not even Jason anymore. What are we if we're not a real family?"

"I want a wife," he said, dropping the mail back on the table. "I want someone to share my life with, someone to talk to."

"We talk," I said.

He shifted from one foot to the other. "I know, but …" His voice trailed off.

"I mean, I thought we had a deal. I could tell you anything and you could tell me anything."

"And I don't want you to stop talking to me," Dad said. "It's just that … I'm the parent … I don't think it's appropriate for me to be telling you so much." He held up a hand like he was trying to block any objection I might make. "And I know it's my fault. I told Anne that."

My Greek salad began to burn in my stomach. "What do you mean, 'told Anne'? Told her what?"

"I asked her opinion, that's all."

"She doesn't even know me," I said. My voice sounded sharper and louder than I'd meant it to.

Dad blew out a breath. "You're missing the point," he said. "For God's sake, Izzy, you're sixteen years old and you know everything about my life."

"And you know everything about mine. So?"

"I'm your father. It's too much information."

I wrapped one arm around myself. "Is that what you think? Or is that what Anne thinks?"

He shook his head. "We're completely offtrack here. This has nothing to do with Anne."

Nothing to do with Anne? I almost asked what color the sky was in his world.

"It has everything to do with her," I said. I was breathing hard, trying not to scream at him. "You never had a problem with us talking about stuff before. You never wanted to get married again. And you were happy—or at least that's how you acted."

"People change. I've changed. I told you that," he snapped. A vein in his left temple pulsed. "I love Anne. And I want us to be a family the way it used to be. That's not wrong."

"The way it used to be," I snorted. "You mean Mom and Jason and me, 'cause you were never around."

"Stop right there," he shouted. His arm whipped out and one finger pointed at me. "I have listened to you, now you listen to me. It's my life. I love Anne. She loves me. I'm going to marry her."

I could hear the blood rushing in my ears. I didn't say anything. I didn't trust my mouth to be able to string words into sentences.

The silence seemed to push us farther apart. I thought about jumping up and launching myself, wailing and flailing, at him. But I didn't. I think about doing those kinds of things, but I never follow through. I don't know if I'm too practical or too chickenshit.

"I have some work to do," Dad said finally, in a flat voice. "I'll see you in the morning."

I stared at a chair instead of him.

"We're not done," he said from the doorway.

I looked down at my right hand. The two pages of script I'd been holding were twisted into a mangled paper rope.

I felt the same way.

5

I sat on the radiator in Mrs. Taylor's English class, trying to soak up some heat. Inside, the pipes clanged and banged and shook, but all that came out were little puffs of barely warm air. Behind me, rain hit the windows, pooled into little rivers and ran down the glass.

Lisa dumped her backpack onto her desk and dropped into her seat. "My feet are wet," she grumped, undoing the laces of her boots and kicking them off. "Why don't they cancel school on mornings like this? Why don't they cancel life?"

She stretched her legs into the aisle. She was wearing hot pink-and-orange-striped socks with individual toes—like gloves for your feet. She'd gotten them for fifty cents at the Sally Ann. On her they worked. On me they would have clashed with my hair.

"You know this?" Lisa asked, yawning.

"I guess so." I fished an elastic out of my own bag and pulled my hair back into a ponytail. It was getting curlier by the second. "What about you?"

"What's to know? It's English. You write a lot about symbolism, allegory, how everything means something else."

"Or nothing."

"Yeah, well don't write that down," Lisa said. "It's not what Mrs. T. wants to hear."

Lisa and I had been friends since third grade, when I caught Matthew Hetherington trying to look up her dress while he gave her an under-duck on the swings. She was my fun friend—the absolute best person to hunt for retro stuff with at the thrift store or to go with to get your ears double pierced.

That was the way my friends were. They all fit into some category, like movie friends or honors math friends.

Lisa yawned again, then leaned her head against the wall and closed her eyes.

"What's with you this morning?" I asked.

"I stayed over at my dad's," she said. "The munchkins got up at five and guess whose bed they climbed into? One second I'm asleep and the next I've got sticky fingers yanking my eyelids up."

"Does it bug you?" I leaned back until my own head was against the window frame and hoped the question sounded casual. "I mean, that your dad got married again and everything?"

"Nah. Andrew and Sam are cool little guys most of the time and I like Haviland okay, even though I think her name sounds stupid."

"What about your mom's husband?"

Lisa opened her eyes and turned her head to look at me.

"You're kidding, right? I haven't bought a CD or a concert ticket since my mom met Sean. I got to meet Keith Dunst of Technical Virgins. If my mom and Sean ever split up I'd go live with him."

She put her hand on the radiator. "Geez, haven't the prisoners started shoveling coal down in the dungeon yet? Oh, I forgot." She put a hand to her cheek in fake surprise. "They have to write an English test first."

I rolled my eyes at her.

For a second I considered telling Lisa about Dad wanting to marry Anne, even though it wasn't the same as her family at all. For one thing, Lisa's mother wasn't dead. Her parents were even friends. And her father was nothing like mine. Lisa's dad drove a minivan. He'd never missed a single school concert or parent-teacher night or anything Lisa'd been in. I'd bet he'd never stayed out all night. Plus Lisa liked what's-her-name—Haviland. I didn't even know Anne.

It wasn't the same. Not at all.

6

"Can't sleep?"

I started and squealed like a bagpipe with asthma. "Jason! Don't do that."

He grinned. "Sorry." But I knew he wasn't.

"Look what you made me do." The spoon was sinking in the pot of spaghetti sauce.

Jason tossed his leather jacket over the back of a chair. "I'll get it. I'll get it," he said, elbowing me away from the stove.

He stuck his head over the pot. "Mmmm, smells good. I'm starving." Then he reached in and grabbed the spoon. It was about to go under for the last time. "Oww! Hot! Hot! Hot!" The spoon clattered onto a burner, spraying drops of sauce everywhere.

I whacked him on the arm with the back of my fist. "Get out of the way and don't help me." I dropped the dirty spoon in the sink and got another from the drawer.

Jason was waving the fingers on his right hand in the air. "I'm hurt," he protested.

"Run them under some cold water," I said. He pushed past me and I couldn't help it; I checked his face, his eyes, half expecting him to grab the spoon out of my hand and start eating the sauce right out of the pot.

I remembered Jason sitting behind me on the counter once when he was wrecked, eating marshmallows because they were the first things he touched. He pulled the bag open in the middle and ate them one after the other, talking really fast the whole time. Nothing he said made any sense and I could see the white goo stuck all over his teeth.

I didn't eat marshmallows for a long time after that.

But Jason didn't look stoned this time. Jason hadn't been stoned for quite a while. So why did I hold my breath whenever he walked in? Why did I check his eyes, smell his clothes, count the number of times he wiped his nose?

He sat in the chair opposite me and slid down so his long legs were under the table and his head was against the back of the chair. His hair was the same color as mine these days, but cut short and spiked. I could feel his blue eyes on me. Spencer appeared and jumped into Jason's lap. Jason gently stroked the fur under the cat's chin. Spencer's eyes closed and he began to purr. Traitor.

Jason sat there looking at me, with his cocky smirk, not saying anything until finally I looked at him. Which he knew I would. He'd been doing that since I was four and he was seven.

"So where were you last night?" I demanded.

He arched his head back and laughed. "Working. How was dinner?"

"Working? At 6:30? What were you doing? Playing dinner music at the Holiday Inn?"

"Good one, Iz." He licked his index finger and made an imaginary mark in the air. "I'm teaching a music class for kids."

"You're kidding."

He shook his head. It was possible, I decided, although I was having a hard time picturing Jason as a teacher. Then again, he'd know every scam and excuse for getting out of practicing.

"So? What was the big dinner out all about? It's 11:30 at night and you're cooking." He paused. "Something's wrong," he added in a singsong voice.

I stopped stirring. "He didn't tell you, did he?"

"All I got was a message that Dad wanted us all to have dinner. Actually I think it was three messages."

I took my time, looking all around the room as though I was trying to find something, before I dropped the words, "Dad's getting married."

"Of course he is," Jason said.

"He's probably asked her by now." I gave him a big, fake, chipmunk-cheeked grin. "Dinner was your chance to meet the bride. I think you blew your shot to be ring bearer."

Jason sat up straighter. "God, you're serious." His mouth moved but it took a few moments for more words to come out. "Why? Who's the her?"

"Her name is Anne McGwire and I barely know her so I can't tell you much. She works on the show and no, she's not the blond."

"Too bad. She's hot."

I shot him my eat-dirt-and-die look, then turned the heat off under the sauce and leaned against the stove. "As for why, Dad says he wants a real family, and you and me and him aren't that. He wants a partner, someone to talk to."

"Shit! He had to marry Mom twice for it to take. What is this? Some kind of midlife thing?"

I shrugged.

"Why can't he buy a motorcycle? I could borrow that."

"Hey, Jason," I said. "Here's an idea. Why don't you pretend to be my big brother and listen to me?"

"I am listening," he said, but I knew all the little gears and belts and wheels were turning behind his eyes as he tried to figure out if Dad getting married was going to mess up his life in any way.

"Have I done a bad job?" I asked. It was the question that had been floating in my mind since Dad had first said he wanted to marry Anne.

"You mean around here?" Jason said. "No. You're practically perfect, Izzy. You can do everything." He held out his arms. "Look at this place. There're no pizza boxes on the back of the toilet. There're no stinky socks in the middle of the table."

"That's because we're not at your apartment."

He nodded. "Yeah. Here there's milk in the refrigerator you can actually drink and extra toilet paper and clothes you don't have to smell before you put them on. You have Band-Aids, for God's sake."

"It's not enough for Dad. He says we can't talk to each

other anymore. He says it's 'not appropriate.'" The words seemed to stick on my tongue.

Spencer flopped onto his side and Jason began to scratch behind the cat's ears. The purring got louder. "I've always thought it was a little weird the way you talk to Dad about everything," Jason said. "I sure wouldn't do it. But I don't get what's not appropriate about it. There have to be dozens of books out there on how to get your kid to talk to you."

I rocked back and forth on the balls of my feet, pushing off from the edge of the stove.

"So he wants to marry this Anne-person so he'll have someone to talk to?"

I shrugged. "I guess. And you know how he is. That'll last for about a month and then he'll disappear for three days looking for fifty-year-old oak boards."

"Did you say anything to him?" Jason asked. Spencer sounded like a truck with a bad muffler.

"Yeah, I said something, for all the good it did."

"So—I don't know—tell him if he gets married you'll, you'll get your tongue pierced."

I shuddered. "Yeech! I would never do that!"

"Right. I forgot I'm talking to Miss Perfect." He ran a hand over his hair. "Tell him you'll run away." He gave me a sly grin. "Tell him you'll quit school and move in with me."

"I would rather French the old guy with green teeth who walks around downtown with his 'The end is near' sign, only he spells near with two es, than move in with you," I said.

"Well, what do you want me to do? It's not like he'll listen to anything I say," Jason said. "Look, it's his life. He has the right to screw it up any way he wants. So he marries whatever her name is and it doesn't work out. They'll get divorced. It's not like you're five years old or something. What's it to you?"

I closed my eyes for a second and shook my head. "I'm the one who has to live here when people start screaming and clothes end up all over the lawn."

Jason shrugged. "Sorry, Iz, but the rest of us don't do everything as perfectly as you do."

"It's not about being perfect, Jason." I was almost spitting the words. "It's about thinking things through before you do something stupid. It's about not screwing up everyone else's life when you screw up your own."

I felt like I could hear my own anger buzzing in the silence. Jason gave me a long, appraising look and shook his head. "Izzy, you think too much sometimes."

I opened my mouth and closed it again. Maybe I did think too much. But it was only because everyone else in the family didn't seem to think at all.

1

"Sssst!" The sound came from behind me, like air whistling out of a balloon. Great. Had the mike picked it up?

"Sssssst!"

So much for this being the Quiet Room at the Seniors Center. I twisted in my chair to mouth "quiet" at whoever was at the door. It was Mrs. Mac. She beckoned to me.

I held up one finger. She nodded and the door closed. I waited for Mrs. Patterson, sitting across from me, to finally take a breath and then I pressed the pause button. **Rule #19: Treat your elders with respect. Someday you'll be old and annoying too.**

"Mrs. Patterson, this is, uh, fascinating," I said, thinking that her soft little voice had most likely been drowned out by Mrs. Mac's hissing. Mrs. Patterson could talk for two paragraphs without taking a breath because she didn't waste any energy on volume. "I just need to check on something."

"That's all right," she said. She patted her hair. "I'll go to the ladies and check my hair."

Check her hair? Her hair never changed. Like Mrs. Mac's, it wouldn't move in a tornado. Mrs. Patterson had a head full of lavender-tinged curls so stiff they could have doubled as a bike helmet.

Mrs. Mac was waiting in the hall. "I'm sorry for interrupting, dear," she said, "but the bus will be leaving soon."

"That's okay," I said. "What is it?"

"I need to borrow a screwdriver—a Phillips head. It's the one with a cross, not the one with the little square—that's a Robertson."

"What do you need a screwdriver for?" I asked.

She looked around, leaned forward and whispered, "My toaster oven is on the fritz."

"But doesn't Oak Manor have some kind of maintenance person to fix things?"

"Jerry." Mrs. Mac snorted. "A secret goes in his ear and right out his mouth. And even if it didn't, it would take him at least a week to get around to me, and I only have enough muffins for two days."

She looked at me as though that had all made perfect sense. I'd been hanging around the Seniors Center long enough to know that old people's brains make leaps in logic the rest of us can't follow. I held up both hands. "First of all, you can buy muffins here. And second, what secret?"

Mrs. Mac was already shaking her head. "No, no, no, dear. The ones they sell here are made with wheat bran. It's too hard on Edgar's colon. I use oat bran."

Edgar?

"Who's Edgar?" I rubbed the space between my eyebrows and wondered what it felt like when all the blood vessels in your brain popped.

Mrs. Mac reached for one of my hands and folded her two around it. There were brown liver spots on the backs of her hands and the veins bulged through the skin, but her fingers were strong holding on to mine. "Try to pay attention, dear," she said. "Edgar Jamer. You know. He uses a walking stick instead of a cane and he wears a hairpiece that looks like the backside of a cat." She lowered her voice. "He's not fooling anyone with it."

I let out a slow breath. "And why are you making muffins for him?"

"That's what he has for breakfast. Plus a bowl of fruit and a glass of hot water with lemon." Her voice went to a whisper again. "He has a problem staying regular."

"Why isn't he eating breakfast in the dining room with everyone else?" Mrs. Mac and a lot of the other seniors at the center lived in an assisted living complex. They each had their own small apartments, but all the meals were served in a big dining room.

"Well, having him join us for breakfast wasn't my idea. Sarah showed up with him in tow one morning. She calls him her boyfriend. Isn't that a ridiculous word to use when you're talking about an eighty-four-year-old man?"

I glanced back through the half-open door. Mrs. Patterson, a.k.a. Sarah, was still in the bathroom with her hairspray, enlarging the hole in the ozone layer. "So you're making breakfast for people in your room?" I asked.

"Just Sarah and Edgar. And Barbara Miller. And Edith Turner—I don't think you've met her, dear." She was still holding my hand, and she gave it a squeeze before she let go.

"Why don't you all go to the dining room?" I asked.

She pursed her lips. "They mean well, but…the coffee is always that decaffeinated kind. There's never any sausage or bacon—too much cholesterol. And the eggs aren't even real eggs." She looked at me, defiant. "I'm seventy-nine years old. If I want to be killed by a sausage that's no one's business but mine."

My mouth went into contortions so I wouldn't laugh and I had to cough a couple of times before I could trust myself to talk. "But you're not supposed to be cooking in your room," I finally said. "I get it. That's the secret."

"They have the idea we're a bunch of feeble ninnies who'll set ourselves on fire." It's difficult to look indignant when you're barely over five feet tall, but she was giving it her best effort.

I got a mental picture of Mrs. Mac trying to hot-wire her toaster oven. Not good. "Will you be home tonight?" I asked.

She was already smiling. "Yes."

"I'll be there about seven thirty."

"You are a dear girl," she said, standing on tiptoes to kiss my cheek. She smelled like lavender and those tiny red candy hearts they only sell around Valentine's Day.

I shook my finger at her. "Don't touch that toaster oven."

She gave me a little wave and headed for the lounge with short, fast steps, singing "Start Me Up," just under her breath.

8

"Why am I doing this?" Rafe asked, reaching behind the seat for his backpack.

"Because you're a nice guy," I said as I got out on my side of the car. "Because you used to be a Boy Scout and you never got over that good deed thing. Because you don't want an old lady burning down half a city block." I grabbed his arm and pulled him over sideways so I could kiss his cheek. "And because you love me."

Rafe hiked the backpack onto one shoulder and put his free arm around me. "I'm not sure I can fix it," he said.

"I don't care about that," I said, leaning into his body and matching my steps to his as we walked. "I just don't want Mrs. Mac trying to do it and then ending up setting this place on fire."

"You like her."

"Yeah, I do. She never talks about her 'ailments' or complains that all the kids today are on drugs. You should hear how some of the old people at the center talk."

We walked through the double doors into an area that reminded me of a hotel lobby. "We're here to see Rose McKenzie," I said to the woman behind the fake marble counter.

"She's in 308," the woman said, giving me one of those not-quite-real smiles you get from people who have jobs that require them to be pleasant all day. She pointed. "Just take the elevators over there."

The door to Mrs. Mac's apartment was a glossy dark blue. Across the hall the door was peapod green, and farther down I could see one that was shiny yellow. Was that so nobody ended up in the wrong apartment?

I rang the doorbell. There was a tiny wreath of red berries around the peephole. In a moment Mrs. Mac opened the door. "Hello, dear," she said. Her smile was the warm, real kind that made you smile back. "Did you bring it?" she whispered.

"Even better," I said, grabbing Rafe by the sleeve and pulling him next to me. "Mrs. McKenzie, this is my boyfriend, Rafe."

"Hello, Rafe," she said, turning toward him.

"Hi," he said, already charmed.

She gestured at the backpack. "Are those your tools?"

He nodded.

"Got a soldering iron in there?" She lowered her voice to a whisper again and laid her hand on his arm.

Rafe grinned. "Uh-huh."

"What else?" she asked, looking up at him, her head cocked to one side.

For a second I got a flash of how beautiful she must have been when she was young. And then I realized she was flirting with Rafe. He seemed to like it.

I followed them into the apartment. They were talking about elements and voltage meters and Phillips head screwdrivers. I was pretty much being ignored.

I kicked off my shoes and wandered around. Like Mrs. Mac, the place was small and warm. There was a tiny blue flowered sofa, heaped with bright pillows, and a matching chair at one end of the room. A round wooden table and four chairs sat next to the window.

The kitchen was just a small stretch of counter with an equally small sink and a few cupboards. The fridge was the kind you'd find in a motel room.

There were pictures everywhere—on a small, square table between the sofa and the chair, along one wide window ledge— of her children and grandchildren I guessed: a chubby baby with mushed peas spiking his hair like gel, a little girl with her arms flung around Mrs. Mac's neck, their faces pressed together. And me. There among all the other pictures on that little table was one of me, in a small pewter frame. It had to have been taken at the center. I turned around. "Mrs. McKenzie, where did you—"

"That's it," Rafe proclaimed. He propped an elbow on the countertop and grinned at Mrs. Mac.

"Splendid," she said, clapping her hands together.

"That was fast. What is it?" I asked, forgetting about the photograph.

"Just needs a new element," Rafe said. He looked at his

watch. "You know, Eastman Supply doesn't close until nine o'clock. I could just zip over there and they might have one. It'll only take me ten minutes."

He was already pulling on his jacket. "Be right back," he added as the door closed behind him.

"I like him," Mrs. Mac said, turning to me.

"I know," I said. "You were flirting."

"I was not," she said, but she couldn't keep from smiling. She moved toward the sofa. "Come sit down."

I sat next to her. She reached over and gave my cheek a little pat. "Thank you so much for helping me, Isabelle. I didn't know how I was going to manage breakfast."

"They could go to the dining room," I said.

"I suppose this all seems kind of silly to you," she said. "A bunch of crotchety old people who have to have their breakfast just so."

"You could never be crotchety," I said. "And I'll tell you a secret. I've been eating the same breakfast since I was four. Shredded wheat and banana."

"We're all creatures of habit in one way or another, my dear."

"Isn't it a lot of work for you?" I asked, curling one leg and a sock foot underneath me.

"I'm just baking a few muffins and scrambling an egg or two," she said. "It gives me a purpose. Keeps me from staying in bed half the day. And then I listen to everyone go on about their aches and pains and I see that I'm in pretty good shape for my age."

"I hope I'm just like you when I'm your age."

She leaned over and hugged me. All of a sudden there was a big lump in my throat that I had to swallow twice to get down.

"So where did you get the picture of me?" I asked.

She reached over and picked up the frame. "Edgar Jamer took that. He used to be a photographer for the newspaper." She hesitated. "You don't mind me having it, do you?"

I shook my head. "I'm...honored." I could feel the lump again. "Who are all these other people?" I asked, gesturing at the table.

Mrs. Mac pointed to the baby with the punk rock hair. "That's Dustin, my newest grandson. And the picture next to it is his sister, Emily Rose."

We were still looking at the photographs when there was a soft tap and Rafe leaned around the door. He had a big guess-what-I've-done smirk on his face.

"You found one," Mrs. Mac exclaimed.

Rafe stuck out his arm. He was holding a plastic shopping bag. The smirk got even bigger and he nodded.

"Well, then, let's get started." Mrs. Mac was already on her feet.

I hugged my knees to my chest and watched the two of them fishing pliers and screwdrivers out of Rafe's backpack. For once there wasn't anything I had to fix. And I thought, Maybe I'll just stay here. Maybe I'll make Rafe and Mrs. Mac my family and I'll just never go home again.

9

I'd pretty much stayed out of my dad's way all week. It wasn't hard. I think he'd been avoiding me too.

When I got home from school Friday afternoon, a dirty white panel truck was in the driveway, the back door rolled up. There was a stack of waffle-patterned pads and a pile of plastic inside.

I dropped my things in the kitchen. I could hear voices. "Drop your end … now let it slide … easy … easy!"

I stepped into the hallway. Two men were bringing a double mattress down the stairs. The guy in front had long hair, mostly gray streaked with dark, pulled back in a ponytail. "Hi," he said when he saw me. He jerked his head toward the front door. "Could you get that for us?"

"Sure." I swung the door open and stepped out to hold the screen.

"Ready? Lift," Ponytail said to the guy in the rear as he got to the bottom step. "Thanks," he added as he passed me. Then, "Careful, there are seven steps here," to his helper. *He* had shaggy blond hair and lots of intriguing bulges in his red plaid shirt. He gave me a once-over. I gave it right back and he almost tripped on the second step.

"Hey, watch it, Paul," Ponytail called out sharply as the mattress listed to the right.

Paul gave me an embarrassed grin and I grinned back. I watched them move across the lawn to the truck. I watched the way Paul's shoulders moved as he lifted. And suddenly I remembered that two men I had never seen before were putting furniture from my house into their truck.

I looked back into the house. Dad was partway down the stairs carrying a couple of long metal things.

"What's going on?" I asked.

He waited until he was level with me before he answered. "They're from the shelter. I gave them the bed."

"What bed?"

"Mine." He didn't look at me. "I have new stuff for the bedroom."

"You mean for Anne." So he must have asked her and she must have said yes.

"Yes. The big chest and the headboard are in the basement. They're yours whenever you want them." Dad handed the two metal rails to Ponytail, who thanked him and headed back to the truck.

"What about Jason?"

"It's okay with him."

"Uh...thanks, then," I said.

I watched while Ponytail covered the mattress with plastic and wrapped a couple of pads around the rails. Paul mostly stood around being decorative, glancing back once in a while to see if I was still watching. I gave him a little wave as the truck drove away.

When I stepped back inside I heard the toilet flush in the upstairs bathroom. In a minute Anne started down the stairs. She was green. Lima bean green, and her lipstick was gone. Another one of my mom's rules popped into my head: **A smile and the correct red lipstick can take off five years**. I was pretty sure Anne didn't want to hear that. She held onto the railing as though the stairs were rocking under her like a boat. She looked like someone who had just puked her guts out.

"Are you all right?" I asked.

"I'm not sure," she said. She tried to smile, but it was mostly just lips stretching. "I think I caught something. It can't be anything I ate. I've hardly eaten all day."

I backed up a few steps. I didn't want to catch whatever germ she had.

Dad suddenly appeared beside me. "Anne, what's wrong?" he asked. He reached out to touch her. She wrapped one arm around her stomach and waved him back with the other hand.

"It's just my stomach, Marc," she said.

"Do you need a doctor? Can I get you anything? Do you want to lie down for a while?" I'd never seen my father make so much fuss over someone heaving her cookies. A thought began to buzz in my head, like a mosquito hovering around my ear.

Anne shook her head. "I'd just like to go home."

"Okay, I'll take you." Dad's hands hovered all around Anne.

I stood there and listened as the car drove away and my own stomach slowly sank to the floor. *No way*, a voice in my head kept saying. *No way*. I grabbed my bag, fumbled in the bottom for my keys and used them to lock the front door behind me.

I started walking, faster even than I usually went. I could hear the blood rushing in my ears, or maybe it was the ocean.

10

Rafe was out running. The entire hockey team was out running up hills and through the trees in Ashburn Park. Cross-training. Jennie Watkins told me.

Great. Why couldn't he be chasing a puck up and down the rink? Or working on surreptitiously hooking someone's skate blade with his stick? Or even practicing his "Who me?" face for the referee?

I needed Rafe. I needed someone to tell me I was wrong—small-minded, suspicious and wrong.

Lisa wasn't around either. She was at the radio station doing something for Sean, her stepfather.

I watched Jennie run the stairs at the gym, from the floor to the nosebleed section, working a wad of gum like some bionic cow chewing its cud. And I actually had the wild idea, for a second, that I could talk to her. I mean, I've known Jennie since first grade. Back then she used to chew little bits of newspaper with flour-and-water paste when we did papier-mâché.

The idea disappeared faster than my warm breath in the cold gym air. We weren't that kind of friends.

I could have just gone home, waited around and talked to Dad. Let him see the slimy, suspicious thing inside me. That thought hung around a lot longer, but then it stretched out to nothing. I couldn't talk to him. Not because there was a chance I might be wrong, but because I was pretty sure I was right.

I heard Jason before I saw him. I stopped on the sidewalk and let people move past as the music came toward me. It was just Jason's voice and his guitar, and for maybe the millionth time I thought how beautiful his music was.

He was usually in front of the downtown liquor store on Friday. The manager had run Jason off the sidewalk three times and threatened to have him arrested. Then people coming into the store on Fridays started asking where Jason was. Now he sat right next to the doors.

There were maybe fifteen or so people listening to him, all stockbroker–investment-banking types that worked in the office building next to the liquor store. I knew he wouldn't stop until he was ready, but I edged around until I was standing in his line of sight. He finished one song and went right into another. All I got was that Mr. Spock from the old-time *Star Trek* thing he does with one eyebrow. He's such an asshole sometimes. Jason, I mean.

When he was finished, everyone clapped, even me. Most of them dropped something in Jason's guitar case. There was at least as much paper money as there were coins.

I walked over to him. "Good day?" I asked as he shoved the bills into one pocket and everything else into the other.

He shrugged. "Not bad. What are you doing here?"

"I need to talk to you."

"What about?"

"Dad."

Jason snapped the last clasp on the guitar case and stood up. "So what did he do now? Did he and chickie-poo elope or something?"

"Her name is Anne," I said. "Jason, I just need to talk to you."

"I need something to drink first," he said.

I flinched. I couldn't help it.

"Jesus, Izzy. Coffee. I need some coffee and something to eat. I didn't have any lunch." Jason leaned forward and exhaled in my face. "See, nothing but the evils of bad breath." He picked up the guitar case. "C'mon. Let's go to Casey's. I don't want to hump this thing any farther than I have to."

He handed me his backpack and I slipped it over one shoulder. We headed down the street to Casey's Diner.

"Hey, is this about the bed?"

"It's not about the bed." I hiked the backpack up a little higher. It was heavy and something clinked inside. "What's in here?" I said.

"Stuff for my kids' class. We're making musical instruments. Drums, shakers, things like that."

"You like it?"

"You mean the class? Yeah." He stopped for a second and switched the guitar to his other hand. "Little kids, they don't care about keeping perfect time or being in tune. All they care about is making lots of noise and having fun."

We were at the diner then. It was almost empty. Jason slid into a booth against the wall and set his guitar case on the floor. I sat across from him.

A waitress appeared and set a cup of coffee in front of Jason. "The usual?" she asked.

"Please," he said. He gave her that smile he does, the one that could make a woman on her deathbed sit up and shave her pits. It's worked on every woman Jason's ever met. Except Mom. And me. I guess if you were related to him you had some kind of genetic immunity.

The waitress had to be at least fifty, and I swear she was blushing when she turned to me. "What can I get you?" she said.

"Large fries with extra gravy and a large milk," Jason said.

"Small milk," I said, giving him a squinty-eyed glare. Maybe I didn't have a smile that made people drool, but I did a great glare.

Jason slouched against the green vinyl seat. "So, what's going on?"

As soon as I said it, it wouldn't be a "maybe" idea floating in my head anymore. It would be real. Or at least a real suspicion. I took a deep breath and then I just said the words. "I think Anne's pregnant."

"Holy shit," Jason said. Then he started to laugh.

Now I'd finally said it out loud, I had to say all of it. "She was at the house when they were moving the bed and stuff. Except she was upstairs puking." Jason was still laughing. "Will you stop that," I snapped.

He took a gulp of coffee. "Sorry. It's just that Dad's always been paranoid I'd knock up some girl and now *he* has." He couldn't get rid of the smirk. "Though I suppose it could be the flu or something."

"I don't think so. When we went to dinner she didn't have any of the wine."

"There are other reasons people don't drink, Izzy."

"But Dad must have told her about you…and stuff. If she'd had a problem, wouldn't she say so?"

"Nah, sometimes we just do the secret addict handshake with each other and leave it at that."

The waitress showed up then with our food. The French fries were homemade, nearly floating in rich, brown gravy. I grabbed one and let the gravy drip onto my tongue before I shoved it in my mouth. It was almost as good as when Rafe slid his tongue in my mouth.

I picked up my fork. **Fingers do not belong in your nose or on your plate. Rule #9.** Or maybe it was **Rule #10.**

Jason's usual turned out to be a hot chicken sandwich with a side of coleslaw. For a few minutes we just ate. Then Jason said, "What if she is pregnant? It's not the worst thing in the world."

"What if she did it on purpose, so he'd have to marry her?"

Jason set down his fork. "She didn't 'do it' by herself. And it's not 1963, Izzy. They don't have to get married." He pushed his plate away and leaned against the back of the booth again. "Maybe she is pregnant. Maybe they planned it. Maybe it was an accident. Accidents happen. You have been paying attention in sex ed, haven't you?"

"I've known about sex since I was six," I said. "I'm the one who explained it to you."

"So you know protective garments have been known to fail," Jason said. "Anyway, all you have to do is wait for a few months and then you'll know one way or the other."

"I don't want to wait for six months or nine months or whatever until Dad says, 'Here's your baby brother or sister.' I want to know now." I pushed my own plate aside. The last few fries were soggy.

"Okay, so they're getting married because she's pregnant, not because Dad wanted someone to talk to. That should make you feel better."

"Well, it doesn't."

"C'mon, Dad has to have learned something from having you and me. Maybe he won't screw it up." Jason stretched his arm along the back of the booth. "What's that saying? Third time lucky."

"More like here we go again," I muttered.

"Anyway, look at it this way. Dad will be so busy with a new wife and a new kid you'll be able to do whatever you want."

I thought about leaning across the tabletop and jamming my fork right in the middle of Jason's forehead. "You mean I'm going to start acting like you?" I said instead.

He gave me a snarky look. "You? The perfect child starts acting like Jason the screwup? Right, like that'll happen."

"I'm not trying to be perfect, Jason," I said, working to keep my voice down when what I really wanted was to scream at him. "I'm just trying to keep Dad from doing something I know is going to be a disaster. You know, it wouldn't kill you to think about someone else besides yourself once in a while."

He laughed. "I couldn't do that. I'm too selfish to do anything like that. Anyway, it gives you the chance to look even better because I'm such a bad boy."

I stood up. This was stupid.

"Hey, Izzy, don't get mad. Where are you going?"

"I'm not mad." And I wasn't, really. I'd stopped getting mad at Jason about the tenth time I'd found myself sitting beside him on the bathroom floor while he woofed his cookies, holding on to him so he wouldn't pitch headfirst into the toilet bowl and drown.

I pulled on my jacket, found a ten in my bag and set it on the table.

"You don't have to do that," Jason said. But he didn't push the money back at me.

If I wanted to know whether Anne was pregnant, I had to ask someone who knew. And I couldn't see myself stopping by her apartment to say, "So, are you knocked up?"

Dad was the only person I could talk to. Appropriate or not.

11

the house was empty when I got home. I grabbed a handful of
chocolate chip cookies—the last ones from the batch
Mrs. Mac made to celebrate Rafe fixing her oven. I didn't
really want them, but I lay with my feet against the back of
the sofa and my head on the floor and ate them anyway. I
cranked up the stereo until the loose pane of glass in the
antique wooden cabinet on the wall above the right speaker
just barely started to rattle.

I looked over at my mother's picture in the middle of
the mantel. It had been taken out at the lake the fall before
she died. She was squinting a bit into the sun, but she had
that smile she always seemed to have, sort of like she had a
secret, but if you came and sat down beside her she'd share
it with you.

"You would know what to do," I said to the picture. Then
I felt dumb because, number one, I was talking to a picture,
and number two, if my mom had been here, none of this
would've been happening.

Finally Dad came in. I pulled my legs down off the back of the sofa, sat up and aimed the remote at the stereo to ease down the sound. "Hi," I said. "Is Anne okay?"

"She's all right," he said. He sighed and looked at his watch. "I'm going to order a pizza. I don't feel like cooking."

"Sure. How about the vegetarian with bacon?" *You're stalling*, a little voice said in my head.

"It's not a vegetarian if it has bacon," he said. He always said that.

"I know," I said. "But if you order the vegetarian and get them to put on the bacon, you get more vegetables." I always said that.

Dad shook his head and reached for the phone. "Call me when it gets here," he said when he'd hung up. He stuck a twenty under the edge of the telephone and started for the stairs.

Do it, the voice said. "Dad?"

"Yeah?" He half turned, but he was still moving toward the steps.

"Is there anything I should know?" That was so lame I realized as soon as the words were out.

Dad at least had enough guilty conscience to get a little red in the face. "What do you mean?" he asked. Which wasn't what he should have said.

Was this how it was going to be with Anne in our lives? No one saying exactly what they meant? No way was I letting that happen.

"Is Anne pregnant?" Couldn't get any more exact than that.

He swung around. "I thought you might figure it out." At least he wasn't trying to lie.

"Well the puking up was a dead giveaway."

Dad sat on the edge of the rocking chair by the fireplace.

"Were you going to tell me?" I asked. "Or were you going to wait until the baby got here and tell me it was one of those happy-face-price-rollback deals at Wal-Mart?"

"Of course I was going to tell you."

I hugged my knees to my chest. "Then why didn't you? Why did you tell me all that stuff about wanting someone to talk to? Why didn't you just say, 'She's pregnant and I'm going to marry her'?"

"Wait a minute." He held up both hands. "I didn't find out that Anne was pregnant until yesterday."

"When did Anne find out?"

"Yesterday. As soon as she knew, she told me."

I don't have a good poker face. I think it's because I roll my eyes whenever I hear crap.

Dad raked both hands back through his hair, which always meant he was in danger of losing his temper. This was when Jason always threw out his chest and went into his announcer spiel: "Ladies and gentlemen, please proceed in an orderly fashion to the nearest exit. The building must be evacuated immediately. Remain calm. There is no need to panic."

It was his snarky little way of saying Dad was about to blow, and it always pissed Dad off. Which made the whole thing kind of funny. I mean, Jason did this hilarious voice and Dad knew it was coming but he always got mad anyway.

Dad sighed and closed his eyes for a second. Then he said, "When Anne told me about the baby, she also told me she wouldn't marry me. She didn't want me to feel trapped."

If I hadn't been holding on to my knees I would have fallen over in wobbly relief.

Dad kept on talking. "I told her that I loved her and I wanted to marry her and I would camp out on the sidewalk in front of her building in my tent and serenade her on my ukulele until she said yes."

"You don't have a tent or a ukulele," I said, feeling something inside me start twisting into a knot.

"I know. Your brother isn't the only one who can do a melodramatic moment."

"And?"

"And the wedding is still on."

I looked down at my socks, the funky happy-face ones I'd gotten at the downtown thrift store with Lisa.

Dad couldn't stand the silence very long. "I love Anne," he said, so quietly I could hardly hear the words. "She makes me laugh. I can say anything to her. She makes me feel that I can still have a life. After your mother, I wasn't sure I'd ever feel that way. And as for the baby, yeah, I want to be a father again. I'm not that bad at it, am I?"

I could actually feel the warmth of his gaze on me. "C'mon, Izzy. Give it a chance. We can be happy."

The thing was, I thought we already were. I thought *we* could talk about anything. I thought I made him laugh and I thought Jason did too, even if he did piss Dad off sometimes. I thought we were his life. I had to bite the inside of my cheek to get the tears to stay back. When I was sure they would, I looked at him. "You say we'll be happy, but that means you," I said. "You don't know what makes me happy— or even what makes Jason happy. I'm happy in this life. Now. I don't want a new life and I don't want a new family."

The doorbell rang. Dad started at the sound.

I scrambled over to the phone, grabbed the twenty and bolted for the door. I took the box from the delivery guy and gave him the twenty. "It's okay. Keep it," I said.

"Hey, thanks," he said. "Have a good night."

Yeah, right.

Dad was on his feet. I kept the pizza box out in front of me. I wanted to keep him out of my space.

"Isabelle, please just give Anne a chance. She's a wonderful person and she's going to be a great mother."

There was a loud buzzing sound in my head, as though I'd been surrounded by a swarm of wasps. Everything felt strange all of a sudden. My father had turned into someone I didn't know, a stranger, a space zombie. I had a flash of flinging the pizza, sending it whipping through the living room like a Frisbee. But I was still me, and I didn't do things like that.

"Looks like you've got everything you want," I said.

There was something lost and sad in the way he looked at me then. My legs were shaking. I set the pizza box on the chest by the door and went upstairs, gripping the railing as though it was the only solid thing left in my life.

12

"Something's wrong," Rafe said after I'd been in the car about a minute. I'd called him as soon as I heard Dad head for his workshop, said, "Please come and get me," and then hung up.

"Just drive, please," I said. I slid to the middle of the seat, fastened the lap belt and leaned my head against Rafe's shoulder.

"Can we go out to the lake?" I asked.

"You got your key?"

I put my right hand in the pocket of my jacket and shook my key ring. Rafe moved the old Crown Victoria into the left-hand lane. After a few more minutes I said, "Anne's pregnant."

Rafe shot me a quick glance. "You're kidding."

"No." I twisted sideways in my seat belt so I could look at him. I loved looking at him. He had the most gorgeous green eyes I'd ever seen. Not blue green or gray green, true green, the way I imagined the ocean looked as you started going down, down below the surface.

"So that's why your dad wants to get married," Rafe said.

"He says it isn't."

"You believe him?"

"I don't know." I shifted a little more and pulled one leg underneath me. "It just seems like an awfully big co-incidence."

Rafe reached for my hand, raised it to his mouth and kissed the back of it.

I snaked my arm across his chest and neither of us said anything for a while, which was okay because I never minded being quiet with Rafe. Anyway, I knew he was thinking, sorting out his own feelings and probably already worrying about mine. That's the thing about Rafe; sometimes he cares too much. It's like everything he feels is just underneath his skin instead of deep inside somewhere, protected, the way the rest of us keep how we feel.

We bumped down the lake road. Rafe stopped at the turn and I got out and undid the lock between the two pieces of chain closing off the driveway. The car crept the last few feet through the trees and out into the clearing by the cottage.

The cottage was my favorite place in the world. It sat into the hill as if the stone foundation had grown out of the ground with the trees all around it. The shingles were the same blue gray as the rock wall where the beach began. It used to belong to my grandparents. Mom's mom and dad. The cottage is how my mom and dad met.

One summer Dad helped build the verandah that runs across the front of the house. He was twenty-one. My mom was nineteen. Eight weeks later he and Mom were married, and pretty soon they had Jason. If you do the math you see that Jason was at the wedding, if you know what I mean.

We walked around the house and climbed halfway down the stairs to the beach. Sitting on the first landing, I leaned into Rafe and he put his arm around me.

"How do you feel about the baby?" he asked after a moment, as though there hadn't been a gap in the conversation.

The baby. My brother or sister. Well, half anyway.

"I haven't thought about it that much," I said. "I'm not good with babies. They're all wiggly and floppy and there's always something coming out of some part of them and it always smells."

"C'mon, they're not that bad."

I turned my head so I could see his face. "How would you feel if your father told you that you were going to have a baby brother or sister?"

The laughter burst out of him. "I'd call all the TV stations," he said. "And I'd call the Pope because it would have to be an immaculate conception. My mother and father aren't romantic."

"That doesn't mean they aren't having sex."

The whole top half of Rafe's body was shaking, he was laughing so hard. "Oh, so what are they doing? Communicating in code? No, no, wait." He waved his hands in the air. "I know, they're doing sign language with their eyebrows."

He pressed his lips together while his eyebrows twitched on his face and his eyes rolled and darted around. Then he slumped back against the step and started laughing again.

I tried to imagine Rafe's oh-so-serious, stick-up-his-butt dad wiggling his eyebrows seductively at Rafe's mother. Okay, so it was funny. I was laughing now too. I waved one hand at him. "You're right. There's no way your parents have sex."

I leaned back as well, my arms propped on the step, and for a couple of minutes we just sat there like that, watching the stars over the lake. I sighed and leaned closer to Rafe. "That first summer after my mother died we didn't come out here at all. Then the day of my birthday Dad dragged—really dragged—Jason out of bed and said, 'We're going out to the lake.' It was so weird being here without her. I could feel her everywhere. I could smell her. When it got dark we had a fire down on the sand. Jason had met some girl and he was down the beach a ways playing his guitar for her. Dad and I just somehow started talking—really talking for the first time in my life."

My voice started wobbling and I didn't know how to stop the tears sliding down my face. I couldn't talk anymore. Rafe held me so tightly it was hard to breathe, but I didn't care.

13

"Isabelle, do you have a minute?" Anne asked, appearing in the living room doorway just as I was about to head upstairs.

In the two weeks since I'd found out about the baby I'd managed to avoid saying anything more than "hi" and "excuse me" to her, and we hadn't spent more than a minute in the same room.

"Uh, yeah, I guess," I said. She looked pale and queasy. And I told myself I was crazy for thinking I could see a bit of a bulge under her yellow sweater. It was too soon.

"I wondered if you had thought about a dress…for the wedding," Anne said.

I hadn't. Because I was trying not to think about the wedding. I shrugged. "Not really."

"I…" She hesitated, cleared her throat and started again. "I'm having my dress made, and if that's something you wanted to do…or I know a couple of places that may have something you'd like as well."

Something I'd like. How could she know what I'd like

when she didn't even know me. I wanted to say, You're my
stepmother, not my friend. And she wasn't even my stepmother yet.

I bit the end of my tongue until I could find the right
words to answer.

"I'm kind of hard to fit," I said. "I think I should stick to
stores I know."

Anne sighed softly. "All right," she said. Then she turned
and went back into the living room.

My stomach hurt, like I'd swallowed something hard and
heavy.

"Why am I taking history?" Lisa asked as we headed down
the main stairs after our last class.

"Because it's a required course," I told her. "Besides, you
know what they say: those who ignore the lessons of history
are doomed to repeat them—in summer school!"

Lisa stuck her tongue out at me. "Very funny."

I leaned on the locker next to hers while she worked the
combination to her lock. "Where do you want to go first?"
she asked, poking her head inside the locker. It gave her voice
a tinny echo. "Goodwill or Sally Ann?"

"Groovy Street," I said.

Lisa's head popped out like a jack-in-the-box. "What?
You're actually going to spend more than ten dollars on
clothes?"

I closed my eyes. "My dad's getting married. I need a
dress."

"Married?" she squealed. "When?"

"Two weeks."

"So, who is she?"

I opened my eyes again. "Her name's Anne. She works on the show with Dad. I barely know her."

"I barely knew Haviland when my father married her," Lisa said, jamming books into her backpack. "That's how I got my leather jacket."

I didn't get what she meant—which happens a lot with Lisa. "Explain please," I said.

"Dad had the whole guilt thing going on." She slammed the locker shut and snapped the lock. "One time he parked in front of this store. I saw the jacket in the window. Next thing I know he's buying it for me."

I shook my head. "I can't see my father buying me a leather jacket just because he's getting married."

Lisa grinned. "Well, he better be paying for the wedding stuff," she said, grabbing my arm and pulling me down the hallway to my own locker.

"Why?" I asked.

"Because after we find you a dress we're going to the mall. If your father's getting married you need slut shoes!"

14

After my mom died, when I went to bed the last thing I'd do was close my eyes tightly and wish for things to be different. Of course they never were, and I knew they wouldn't be. But every night I made the wish. And for a second, every morning, there was the possibility.

So on the morning of the wedding I lay in bed with my eyes closed for a long time. When I finally opened them, the sun was beginning to reach into the bedroom. Outside somewhere a pair of mourning doves cooed to one another. And on the back of the closet door, so it wouldn't wrinkle, was my dress for the wedding.

I found Jason in the kitchen scrambling eggs with what looked to be most of a jar of salsa. "You want some eggs?" he asked.

I scrunched my eyes shut and stuck my tongue out as I passed him.

"If you ate a little protein in the morning it would stabilize your blood sugar and you'd be in a better mood," he said.

I snapped him with my index finger right in the middle of his forehead. "Don't talk to me," I said.

"Or maybe you're just not getting enough sleep," he said, flipping the glop in the frying pan and then gesturing at me with the turner. "You should try a slice of toast with peanut butter and a big glass of warm milk at night. Lots of trypto-phan. It'll put you right to sleep and maybe you'll wake up a little cheerier in the morning." He gave me a big fake toothy smirk.

"Are you staying here tonight?" I asked.

"Yeah, I'm babysitting you while Dad is on his honey-moon. Why?"

"More like me babysitting you." I pushed the start button on the microwave. "That's good. I'm glad you'll be here. I won't have to drag all the way across town to kill you in your sleep."

"Hey, be nice to your big brother," Jason said, dumping his eggs onto a plate and taking a seat at the table. That was another one of Mom's rules. "I know where they keep that picture of you wearing your potty for a hat."

"You okay about today?" Jason asked after a few minutes of silence.

"No," I said. "But it's happening anyway."

"Yeah, I see talking to Dad worked real well." Jason's fork had stopped in mid-air. His mouth was pulled sideways into a sneer.

I finished chewing, set down my spoon and pictured myself dumping the bowl on Jason's head and beating the shredded wheat into his hair with the spoon.

"Gee, maybe I should have gone out to the lake, gotten wrecked, climbed up on the roof and sung 'Tangled up in Blue' while playing a toy guitar with only four strings," I said.

The sneer slipped off Jason's face. He looked away for a minute then faced me again. "Okay, I deserved that," he said.

I picked up my spoon again. "Nothing's going to change this."

"You can move in with me if you want to."

I sucked in a breath and tried to swallow at the same time. Milk and shredded wheat went up my nose. I choked. I coughed threads of cereal across the table, and milk dribbled down my face.

"Move in with you?" I finally managed to wheeze. "Are you serious?"

"And straight." Jason pulled down his lower eyelids with his index fingers. "Don't let the red eyes fool you. I am not wasted—except for lack of sleep. You want to move in with me, you can."

"But wouldn't that …" I waved my hands in the air because I couldn't figure out how to finish the sentence.

"Make me crazy? Ruin my sex life?" Jason supplied as a grin spread across his face. "Yeah. So … it won't kill me."

I swallowed down the lump in my throat that had nothing to do with cereal. Jason didn't act like my big brother very often. Well, okay, never. I shook my head. "It wouldn't kill you, but we might end up killing each other."

He nodded. "Yeah, probably."

I leaned across the table and kissed the top of his spiky head. "Thanks, Jason," I said. Then I got up and rinsed my dishes in the sink. I could feel tears almost ready to fall and I didn't want that to happen.

15

Rule #27: Great-looking shoes are worth the pain. They were more than great-looking shoes. They were fabulous. Sparkly lavender high, high heels that laced halfway up my calf. And I didn't care if my feet hurt. Maybe they would take my mind off everything else that hurt.

I looked at my dress in the mirror again; pale blue with a round neck, no sleeves, and swirls of lavender and purple everywhere. No lace. No ruffles. No frills. I wondered where the last person to own the dress had worn it.

Spencer peeked out of the closet, whiskers twitching. He didn't like all the uproar. For a second I thought about hiding out in there with him. There was a knock at the bedroom door. Spencer retreated again.

Jason stuck his head in the room. "Ready?" he asked.

No. I wasn't ready.

I thought about holding my breath until my face turned purple and my eyes rolled back in my head, or diving under the bed and lying there for the rest of the day in the cool, dusty darkness.

Rule #7: Hiding under the bed won't solve anything. If the dust bunnies don't get you, the vacuum cleaner will. Mom had told me that one the first day of school in grade six. I'd tried to put red streaks in my hair the night before, hoping it would make me look older. (I was still waiting for my breasts to pop out.) The streaks had turned out purple and I think they glowed in the dark.

Mom made me French toast and braided purple and silver ribbons into my hair so the purple chunks would look like I'd done them on purpose.

I looked down at her bracelet on my wrist. "I'm ready," I said, turning around. Jason held out a hand. I was probably about five the last time we'd held hands. I hesitated for a second, then I laced my fingers through his and we went downstairs together.

Dad was in the middle of the living room. He looked incredibly handsome, his freshly shaved face and crisp, white shirt bright against his charcoal suit. "Look at the two of you," he said. "You look great."

"You're looking good too, Dad," Jason said. I'd never seen the dark suit Jason was wearing. With his deep blue shirt and tie, the effect was sort of mobster chic.

"I'm...uh...glad you're both here," Dad said. He glanced at me. "Thank you."

He didn't seem to know what to do with his hands. It was as if he'd suddenly discovered he had them. As if he'd looked down and found these "things" at the end of his arms. Now they were everywhere, tapping and snapping, adjusting his jacket, touching his hair.

"Hey, Dad, why don't I drive?" Jason said.

"Yeah, why not," Dad said, handing over the keys. He looked at me again.

Don't look at me, I thought. You're not leaving me any space to breathe. I'm here in my pretty dress and my sparkly shoes. That's all you're going to get. That's all I have to give.

Somehow we got out of the house and into the car. I leaned my head against the back seat and closed my eyes.

Dad and Anne were getting married at a small inn about half an hour out of the city. It was going to be a very small, simple wedding, no fancy ceremony or reception, just all of us and some of Anne's and Dad's friends. My grandmother, Dad's mother, wasn't coming. She lived in a nursing home in Montreal and she didn't remember things very well. Anne's mother and father were dead, and like Dad, she didn't have any brothers or sisters.

Jason pulled into the parking lot with a little spray of gravel. Peter Gregory came down the steps of the old house. I hadn't known he was coming.

Peter and Dad had been friends since they were in the seventh grade. The last time Peter had been in town was just before Jason went to rehab.

I got out of the car. Peter grinned and said, "Wow!" I smiled and hugged him. He was pretty "wow" himself in a gray suit and black turtleneck with his salt-and-pepper hair and beard.

Peter pulled Dad into a bear hug and then shook hands with Jason. Dad's hands were going again.

"Well, old man," Peter said, "this is your last chance to cut and run."

"Too late," Jason said, grinning and swinging the car keys in the air.

I didn't know anything about getting married, but it seemed to me that Dad should have looked happier. He should have looked happy period, not like a raccoon squatting on the center line, trying to decide which way to run while the traffic whipped by in both directions.

Peter reached into his pocket. "I thought you might need this," he said. He pulled out a brown necktie, shiny, wide and ugly.

"Oh lord, Peter, that's not..." Dad began.

Peter nodded and draped the tie around his neck.

"You kept that damn thing all this time?"

"Truth, I forgot I had it. Laura found it in a box in the basement."

"Excuse me," Jason said, "but I'm pretty sure it's supposed to be old, new, borrowed, blue, not old, ugly, borrowed and brown. And it only applies to the bride."

"You mean you haven't told them the story?" Peter asked, with an ask-me-why-I'm-grinning grin.

"What story?" I said.

"When your father married your mother," he held up one finger, "the first time, he was...well, he couldn't sleep the night before and he...let's say he over-medicated."

Jason shot a look at Dad, and a smirk started across Jason's face.

"The two of us were waiting in this little room in the basement of the church before the ceremony. It just had this one small window, high up in the wall. And Marc was feeling—"

"—hungover?" Jason supplied.

"There's no bathroom. There's not even a garbage can or a paper bag in the room. So he grabs a chair, climbs up, flings up the window, shoves his head out and…you know. The only problem was, when he stuck his head out, his tie sort of flew out too."

Jason's eyes were closed and he was shaking with silent laughter. I could even feel it in myself.

"The minister's wife came in, thank God. She took the tie and washed it in the kitchen sink. Of course there was no way to dry it. So she decided I should give him my tie, because I was only the best man and no one was going to be looking at me.

"And great guy that I was and still am, I did. I stood there, while he got married, with that cold, wet tie around my neck, sticking to my chest through my shirt."

"Why didn't anyone ever tell me this?" Jason asked.

I looked over at Dad. His mouth stretched up in what passed for a smile, but his lips had almost disappeared. And he kept looking away from Peter. He doesn't like this, I realized.

Peter raised both hands. "Wait. That's not the end of the story." He held up two fingers. "Marc and Susan, take two. Four and a half years later. Same church, same tie. Someone brings you down." He pointed at Jason. "Marc lifts you up in the air and you do this precision, projectile puke right on the tie."

"Hey, it's a God-given talent," Jason said with a shrug.

"So there I am, another wedding of your father's, wearing a cold, wet necktie." He turned, smiling, to Dad. "Marc, you will notice this time," he pointed to his sweater, "no tie." He pulled the loose tie off his neck. "But I am prepared."

Dad took the tie and put it in his left pocket. "Thanks, Peter," he said. "I think." He looked around the parking lot. "Is Anne here yet?"

"You're not supposed to see the bride before the ceremony, remember?" Peter said.

"That's an old superstition."

I grabbed Dad's arm before he could head inside. "Maybe Anne believes in it."

I did. At least for that day…sort of. I didn't want to challenge fate, the wedding gods or the great cosmic plan. I didn't want Dad and Anne to get married, but I didn't want the marriage any more doomed than it already was. "How about if I go see if Anne's here. All right?"

Dad turned to look at me. He exhaled so softly I almost missed the sigh. He nodded. "Tell her I…tell her…I'm here."

I picked my way across the gravel, wobbling as my high heels sank down between the little rocks. When I stepped inside the old house a young woman with spiky hair like Jason's leaned around the doorway to the right. She was holding two small pots of yellow roses. Anne was upstairs getting dressed, she told me, first door at the top of the stairs. I held the banister with one hand, my skirt with the other and made my way carefully up the steps. Outside the door I took a deep breath, straightened my shoulders and knocked.

"Come in." Anne was standing in front of a long oval mirror. She turned, her eyes widening with surprise when she saw it was me. But in the moment before she turned, while she was still looking at her reflection, she'd looked almost as if she was scared, biting the side of her lip.

"You look beautiful, Isabelle," she said.

There was a silence. "You…too," I said, finally remembering my manners.

She did. Her hair had been cut even shorter, and soft bits curled around her face. Her dress was ivory with a tint of pink. It had long, fitted sleeves, a scoop neck and slim skirt.

"Dad just wanted you to know we're here," I said. "And…do you need anything?" I brushed invisible lint off my skirt. Oh Lord, that hand thing of Dad's was catching.

"I don't think so." Anne hesitated. "Except I couldn't do a couple of the buttons at the back of my dress."

"I'll do them. Turn around." The buttons and the loops of fabric that hooked around them were so tiny my fingers felt like they belonged on a giant's hands.

"My fingers are cold," I said. "I'm sorry."

"Cold hands, warm heart."

"Excuse me?"

"It's just something my grandmother used to say, 'Cold hands, warm heart.' She had a lot of sayings like that."

The second button finally slid through its loop. The sun was streaming through the window, making a patchwork of light on the floor. Anne smiled. "She used to say, 'Happy is the bride that the sun shines on, happy is the corpse that the rain rains on.'"

"I guess you're happy then," I said.

She looked straight at me. "Yes, I am. And I hope…I believe we all can be, once we get to know each other. It'll just take some time."

I didn't say anything. Anne broke the silence. "Is your father okay?" she asked.

"He's fine. His friend Peter was telling us this really funny story about Dad, when he and my mom got married. Dad was so nervous he threw up all over his tie."

Maybe it seemed cruel to talk about my mother on that day, but I needed Anne to know that I wasn't going to forget about Mom, not that day, not any day.

Anne crossed over to the bed and picked up a white box. "Could you take these downstairs?" she asked. "There's a boutonnière for your—for Marc, and for Peter and Jason." She hesitated. "And there are flowers for you."

I took the box. "Flowers for me?" I said. "You didn't have to do that."

"I know," she said. "But I wanted to."

I didn't know what to say. That's not something that usually happens to me. And I didn't like the way it made me feel—uncomfortable and uncertain. I had to clear my throat twice before I could get a thank-you out.

"I'll see you downstairs," Anne said. "Thanks for doing those buttons."

I stopped at the top of the stairs and lifted the lid of the flower box. Under the tissue paper was a little bouquet of peach and white roses. My favorites.

The steps shimmered through the tears I was suddenly having trouble holding back. I pressed one cold hand against my face and took some deep breaths. Then I started down.

Rafe and his parents had arrived, along with a bunch of

people from the show. "Isabelle, you look lovely," Rafe's mom said, hugging me.

"Hey, gorgeous," Rafe said. He squeezed my hand, hard. I wished I could have just kept holding on to him.

After that, everything was a blur of words and movement and a fake smile on my face that made my cheeks ache. For the ceremony, Jason and I stood behind Dad. Peter stood next to him.

The minister, a friend of Anne's, stood in front of the fireplace in a long white robe with a blue sash embroidered in gold around her neck. It struck me that her smile was the only one that seemed real.

I concentrated on the sound of the minister's warm, husky voice and tried not to listen to her actual words. But I heard the part about anyone objecting. "Let them speak now, or forever hold their peace," she warned. It was as though she was reminding me, "You can't change it now."

Dad took Anne's hand. The minister looked at Jason. He stepped forward, leaned over and kissed Anne's cheek and laid his hand on top of theirs.

The minister looked at me. I took three steps and put my hand over Jason's. He reached up with his thumb and gave it a squeeze.

"Those whom God has joined together, let no one put asunder," the minister said.

With those words our old family was undone and Dad and Anne were married.

16

they were arguing. Not the screaming, throwing things kind of arguing. This was arguing with low, tight voices. I dropped my pack in the hall and stood in the doorway to the living room. Neither Dad nor Anne had heard me come in. They were standing in front of the fireplace.

I'd spent almost no time at home in the last month and a half. I didn't plan it that way. It's just how it worked out. And all my conversations with Dad—which meant the ones I couldn't avoid—were made up of words with less than two syllables. "How are things?" "Fine." "Do you need any money?" "No."

Anne and I pretty much stayed out of each other's way, except that we always ate breakfast together, me with my cereal and Anne with her dry toast and orange juice. It wasn't my idea. That first morning I came down and she was already at the table. I could feel the awkwardness between us; it was as though there wasn't enough space in the kitchen for both of us. But as the mornings passed I got used to it.

After the first morning there was always a bowl and spoon sitting on top of the microwave for me. We'd sit across from each other and she never tried to talk. I guess she knew that rule. But she always said "Have a good day" as she passed my chair to rinse her dishes in the sink.

"I don't see what's wrong with that," Dad was saying.

Anne sighed and rested one hand on the bump of her belly. "I just think there's room for both pictures," she said.

"I'm not going to put Susan's picture in the basement, Anne. I just want to move it somewhere else."

"Marc, how long has Susan's picture been on that mantel?"

Dad ran his hands back through his hair. Bad sign. "I don't know. Since ... I don't know."

"How do you think Jason and Isabelle will feel, all of a sudden finding that their mother's picture has been stuck off in a corner somewhere?"

"Trust me," Dad said. "Jason won't care and Isabelle will understand. It's not a big deal."

Anne reached up and laid her hand on Dad's shoulder. "Please, Marc. At least wait until Isabelle gets home."

"Isabelle is home," I said.

They both swung around.

"If you're going to talk about me like I'm not in the room, then make sure I'm not in the room," I said. **(Mom's Rule #21.)**

Anne almost smiled. "I'm glad you're here," she said. "Our wedding pictures came back. I'd like to move the photograph of your mother over to the left a little and put a picture of your dad and me at the other end of the mantel. Is that all right with you?"

Sit Mom next to the alabaster elephant she brought back from Mexico, where she could look over at Dad and Anne holding hands? No way. "I'd rather put Mom's picture in my room," I said. "Then you can just put your picture up in the middle."

"Great," Dad said in a too-cheery glad-that's-settled voice.

"Are you sure?" Anne asked.

I nodded.

"You don't have to do that. There's plenty of room for both pictures."

"It's okay. I want to."

Anne looked at me without saying anything for a long, uncomfortable moment. "All right," she said finally. She reached up for the picture and handed it to me. Then she folded both hands over the baby bump. "I have some things to do upstairs," she said, and she left the room without looking at Dad or me.

17

I laid my head against Rafe's chest where I could breathe in the scent of him—deodorant soap and Big Red gum—at the open neck of his jacket. Mixed with the cold night air it was clean and comforting. "Mmm, you smell good," I said.

"You feel good," he said, rubbing one hand down my side and up under one of my sweaters.

I kissed the hollow space at the base of his throat. "Yeah, I've noticed you seem to like the way I feel."

Rafe made a frustrated growl in the back of his throat and pulled me tighter against him. "I don't wanna go."

"What time's practice?"

"Six."

I groaned. "I can't even stand up at 6 a.m., let alone skate." I nipped the curve of his ear with my teeth. "You could skip practice."

Rafe sucked in a sharp breath and let it out slowly. "Stop that," he said. "You want St. Vincent's to take the title this year?" He turned me in his arms so my back was against his chest and leaned his chin on the top of my head. "We could go for breakfast tomorrow after I'm done."

"Can't," I said. "The old gals are having a bake sale at the center and I promised I'd help. They're raising money to buy a van so they can go on some overnight trips."

Rafe laughed. "Overnight in a van. Is it going to have tinted windows and a red velour interior?"

I reached back and gave the side of his head a smack. "Not that kind of overnighter, you sicko. They just want to go shopping and play bingo."

"You don't know that for sure. Even old people get horny sometimes."

I shifted in his arms. "I can't believe you said that. You're the one who's always grossed out thinking about your parents having sex."

He made a face. "That's totally different."

"You want me to believe that some of those old people down at the Seniors Center are …Yeech!"

"Why not?"

I shook my head hard, trying to shake out the picture. "I don't even want to think about it." Great. Now how was I going to look Mrs. Mac in the eye the next time I saw her?

"You're going to get cold out here," Rafe said. "And I should go." He leaned down and kissed me. His lips were warm and my knees went all floppy like a Raggedy Anne doll. I wasn't cold at all. "I really gotta go. I'll call you tomorrow." He gave me one more quick kiss, took the stairs in two giant steps and loped across the lawn to his car.

I watched him drive away, but I didn't go in. I leaned against the railing and looked up at the ink-black sky. It seemed to go up forever. I tried to pick out the Big Dipper. The stars were so bright. The light had made it all this way, but the warmth had been lost millions of miles ago.

An image of old Mr. Jamer, with his dry-clean–only hair, getting horizontal with Mrs. Patterson popped into my mind and I couldn't help laughing.

"What's so funny?" Dad said from behind me.

I started, then turned halfway around. "Just something Rafe said."

Dad came out onto the steps. We watched the sky in silence for a few minutes. "I don't see you much these days it seems," he said, so quietly that for a moment I thought maybe I'd imagined the words.

I didn't even look at him. Was he waiting for me to get all teary? Waiting for us to hug, wipe our eyes and then go inside for cookies and milk? My throat was suddenly tight.

I let my eyes drift sideways. Dad was motionless, looking out at the night sky. Everything between us was different.

"I've been busy," I mumbled.

Then I turned and went inside.

8

Lisa and I were hanging over the second-floor stairwell by the end of the breezeway to the gym. It was a good place to watch people—or to hang out if you wanted people to watch you.

Lisa liked to be noticed. She leaned over the railing as far as she could and rocked back and forth so her butt was in the air. Every guy going past on the stairs looked—which was why she was doing it. "You want to check out Second Coming next weekend?" she asked, smiling down at a skinny guy with shaggy blue and blond hair.

"Aren't you going to your dad's?" I said.

"Nope. He has to go away on business, and Haviland and the small ones are going too." Lisa hung over the railing until her chest was on her folded arms. "You think he's cute?" she said.

"Your dad?"

She screwed up her face at me. "No, stupid. Him." She pointed down the breezeway.

"Nick Dufferin?"

"Yeah. He's in the drama club." She sighed and gave me a moony smile. "I like the sensitive artist type."

"What about Zach?" I asked, leaning beside her.

"Oh please." Lisa rolled her eyes. "That's over." After a couple of minutes she said, "So, how's life with the wicked stepmother?"

I glanced at her, then looked away. "She has all these weird cravings. Like right now it's sour stuff. Either she's eating one of those big pickles from Rye's or she's sucking on those purple sourballs you get from the gumball machine outside the Cineplex. I think my dad's put twenty bucks' worth of change in that thing."

Lisa snorted with laughter. "Haviland's thing was fried clams," she said. "In the middle of the night."

She tugged at the front of her black sweater. "Why couldn't we have fathers like Ashley Cooper's dad. When he turned forty he bought a convertible and had liposuction." She turned to look at me, resting her chin against her shoulder. "Babies aren't so bad though, once they get past the puking up on everything stage."

"Oh great," I muttered.

"No, really, the little critters can be fun. Like last week, I taught Sammy how to shoot a pea right across the table like a spitball. Dad was pissed but Haviland was in the kitchen laughing." She picked at something on the arm of her sweater. "It's not that bad, Iz, honest."

"Sure," I said. "Puke on my clothes and vegetable-spitting contests at the dinner table. In other words, a baby is just like Jason stoned."

"Pretty much," agreed Lisa with a grin.

Whoopee.

19

there was a soft knock at my door. Anne. It had to be. She did everything quietly.

"Come in," I said.

Anne pushed the door halfway open. She was wearing a white cotton shirt with the sleeves rolled up and dark blue pants that hugged her legs, but seemed to magically expand when they got to her middle. She looked to me like she'd swallowed half a basketball. I figured that was how you were supposed to look when you were almost six months pregnant.

"Hi," she said. "I thought maybe you'd like to see a picture of your sister."

"My...? Oh, you mean the baby." I swung my legs around and sat upright on the bed.

She handed me a piece of paper. It looked like a printed picture of TV static. "There she is," Anne said, leaning over the end of the bed to point at a tiny dark blob near the bottom of the picture. "And there's her head, and see those? Those are her legs and her arms."

I stared at the fuzzy image and suddenly I could make out the shape of a baby, with a tiny fist curled against a cheek. It was like staring at one of those drawings that seemed to be just squiggly lines and then all at once became someone's face.

"Hey, I see her," I said.

Her.

I looked up at Anne. She had one arm wrapped around her middle. "You know the baby is a girl?"

Anne smiled. "Yes, that's how it looks. We're going to call her Leah."

I looked at the picture again. I'd never thought of the baby as anything but *it*. I held out the piece of paper.

Anne shook her head. "No. That's for you to keep."

"Uh...no...that's okay." I stumbled over the words. "There must be other people you want to show it to."

"This is a copy," Anne said.

"I don't really have anywhere to put it," I said.

Anne tucked a curl of hair behind her ear and licked her lips a couple of times. "You know, Isabelle, I worry that you're unhappy, that you feel uncomfortable because of me. Because I'm here."

I looked down at my quilt and traced the outline of one of the squares with my finger.

"I know all the changes must feel strange, but if you just give it some time it'll start to feel like your home, your family." She leaned down and set the picture on the bed. "I'll let you get back to studying," she said.

I kept staring at the picture after she left. Now all I could see was a baby. Leah. My sister. I couldn't see just grainy little blobs anymore.

Finally I got up and put the picture, face down, in the bottom drawer of my dresser.

10

I stood in the entrance to the Seniors Center, stomping my feet and shaking off snow like a big old dog.

I'd aced my Communications project. Now I was working on a video about World War Two for my world history class. Rafe said it was just an excuse to keep hanging around with Mrs. Mac and the others, although I noticed he always managed to be there to pick me up on the days they were cooking. Anyway, it was easy for him. He was a good-enough hockey player that he didn't have to worry about marks, even though his were pretty good. I did have to think about things like that. The only sport I played with any degree of ability was mini-golf, and no one handed out scholarships for that.

"There you are," Mrs. Mac said, coming out of the exercise room. She didn't cover much ground in a step, but she moved so fast she'd leave you behind if you weren't paying attention.

She reached up and brushed off the front of my jacket. "Is it still snowing?" she asked.

"Pretty much stopped," I said, holding my hat out at arm's length to shake it. "It was just a flurry."

Mrs. Mac made room for my jacket on the coat rack and laid my mitts over the heating grate in the floor, while I foraged for my sneakers in the bottom of my backpack. She stood with her hands folded in front of her, waiting until I'd tied both shoes before she spoke.

"My dear, I should tell you first that I couldn't truthfully say that Edgar cheats because I haven't seen him do it. And I wouldn't want to accuse him of something I haven't any proof of, you understand."

Not in the slightest.

She continued, "It's just that he seems to win a good many more hands than anyone else. So I don't have a good feeling about leaving the two of them alone for very long—just in case."

"Leave the two of who?"

"Try to pay attention, dear," she said, propelling me down the hall. "Edgar. Mr. Jamer. You know, Sarah Patterson's friend." She rolled her eyes at the word "friend". "And your brother."

"My brother?" I said, stopping in my tracks. "You mean Jason?"

"Yes, dear." She made a hurry-up gesture with her hand.

My feet suddenly seemed to be stuck to the tile floor. "What's Jason doing here?"

"He said he was waiting for you." She laid her hand on my arm. "Is something wrong?"

I didn't know what to say. Of course there was something

wrong. Jason wouldn't be looking for me if everything were okay. I ran down the possibilities in my head. Obviously he hadn't been arrested. He wasn't wrecked because Mrs. Mac would have mentioned that. And no one in their right mind would send Jason to tell me bad news, like something had happened to Dad.

Rule #41: If it's dirty, wash it. If it's hungry, feed it. If it's broke, it's Jason. So he wanted something. Why else did Jason ever look for me? I heard myself sigh. "Where is he?" I said.

"They're in the lounge," Mrs. Mac said.

I followed her the rest of the way down the hall. In the doorway she reached over and gave my arm a little pat. "When I was six I hit my younger brother, Elliot, in the middle of the forehead with a hammer," she said in the same tone of voice she would have used if she'd been offering me a cookie.

"You what?" I turned to look at her.

She gave me a sweet smile. Who'd believe she was capable of braining someone with a hammer? "He was such a tattletale. Always running to Mother," she explained. "And I did warn him." She patted my arm again. "I understand about brothers."

"I bet your brother was nothing like Jason," I said. "He's the older one, but I always end up taking care of him."

"Do you know what Robert Frost wrote about home?" Mrs. Mac asked.

"You mean 'Death of a Hired Man'? We did it last year in English." The conversation was going off on one of those old-people detours.

"My mother said much the same about family. 'When they need taking care of, you have to do it.'"

Easy for her to say. I'd have bet Mrs. Mac's mother never had a family as messed up as mine.

Jason and Mr. Jamer were across the room at a corner table. "Okay son, deal," the old man said. I couldn't help noticing his toupee. Mrs. Mac was right. It did look like a cat's bum.

Jason started dealing cards face up on the table. Mr. Jamer named each one, correctly, just before it was turned over. They were halfway through the deck before Jason noticed me. "Busted," he said, pointing over his shoulder at Mrs. Mac and me. Jason set the cards on the table and stood up. "Thanks," he said, winking at Mr. Jamer, who looked a little sheepish.

"Come on, Edgar," Mrs. Mac said, grabbing him by the elbow and helping him get to his feet. "See you Friday," she whispered as she passed me.

"What do you want?" I asked Jason.

"I don't get 'Hello,' I don't get 'How are you?'" he said.

"Hello. How are you? What do you want?"

"Gee, loosen up, Iz," he said, pulling on his jacket. "I just need to borrow some money."

"You don't look so broke," I said. "That's a new leather jacket."

"Which I bought from one of the guys I've been playing with. Please, Iz. I need some money."

I shook my head.

The charming smile and little boy tilt of the head disappeared. "What do you think I'm going to do, Izzy? Use it to get stoned?"

"I didn't say that."

"You might as well. It's what you're thinking." He shook his head and let out a long breath through his teeth. "I lost my wallet. So I lost all my money and my ATM card. I can't even write a check because all my ID was in my wallet."

I bit down on my back teeth so hard I should have cracked one. My wallet was in the right pocket of my jeans. I gave him all the cash I had. "I'm sorry," I said through my clenched teeth.

Jason shook off the apology. "Forget it." He grabbed his backpack and slung it over one shoulder. "Thanks, Iz," he said, and he was gone.

He hadn't even asked me how I was, or how things were going with Anne and Dad. Did he know yet that the baby had a name? Did he know it was a girl?

I was shivering. I wanted to believe in Jason. But I couldn't seem to get all the way there.

21

It smelled wonderful when I came through the door after school—onions, garlic, tomatoes. I stood in the hall for a minute and breathed it in, then headed for the kitchen.

Anne was at the stove, stirring something in the big spaghetti pot. Spencer was sprawled on the floor in a patch of sunshine under the kitchen window. He lifted his head, but decided I wasn't worth the effort of getting up.

Anne smiled when she noticed me in the doorway. "Hi."

"Hi," I said. "How come you're not at work?"

"We're not taping this week."

"Where's Dad?"

"He went to look at some old doors." She reached for the salt shaker on the counter, shook a little into her hand and dropped it in the pot. "Oak, I think," she said.

I grabbed a green apple from the bowl on the table. "What are you making?" I asked.

"Chicken soup. It's my grandmother's recipe." Anne gestured over her shoulder at a small fabric-covered book lying open next to the sink. I could see spidery writing in black ink on the yellowed pages.

"You're making soup from scratch? Why?"

Anne shrugged. "I don't know. Mostly because I like to." She picked up a knife and started chopping a potato into small chunks.

I took another bite of my apple. "You know, they have chicken soup at the deli," I said after I'd chewed and swallowed. "It's pretty good."

"I'm sure it is," Anne said.

I didn't get it. What was the point of making soup—it was way too much work—when you could just walk to the deli and be back in half an hour with a container of homemade soup?

Anne dropped a handful of potato into the pot and gave it another stir.

I opened the fridge, pulled out a bottle of juice and started for the living room. "My mother always said that's what delis were for," I said. "Bagels and chicken soup." Cooking is for people who haven't mastered take-out.

"But I'm not your mother."

I froze in the doorway. Had I heard the words? Or just imagined them? I looked back at Anne. She gave me a quick glance, with just a hint of a smile. Then she reached for the knife and another potato and started chopping again.

22

I don't know what it was that woke me. Suddenly I was sitting upright in bed as if someone had pushed me from behind, not really awake, wrapped in tangled sheets like a caterpillar in a cocoon.

I listened. And heard something. What? It was a partly stifled moan, low and full of pain. My body froze for a moment; then I was moving, spastic, mostly falling onto the floor with my legs trapped in the twisted covers.

Anne was on her knees in the hall, outside the bathroom door. One hand was braced against the wall, one hand clutched her big belly. The back of her nightgown was soaked and bloody, the wet fabric plastered to the back of her legs. I knew almost nothing about having a baby, but I knew it was too soon to have this one.

"What's wrong?" I asked, squatting on the floor beside her.

Her face was blotched and sweaty. "I think…the baby's coming," she gasped.

"Where's Dad?"

"Out...for the show."

No. No. No. I couldn't scream out loud. I squeezed my hands into tight fists. "Out where?"

"Springfield, I think. To look at...barn board."

Springfield, which was two-and-a-half hours upriver—three if you went on the back roads, which was what Dad had probably done because he was looking for wood from an old barn to make some stupid reproduction cupboard to nail up on a kitchen wall for a "rustic" look instead of being home with Anne and the baby and this whole new family that was supposed to be so hotshot freakin' important that he threw away his old family, and I knew he would do this. I knew it.

All at once Anne's face twisted with pain. She grabbed my arm to steady herself. I dropped down on one knee to keep both of us from going over and put my free arm around her shoulders. Her skin was hot and slick with sweat.

I felt as though an icy hand had pushed through my chest and grabbed my insides, sort of like the creature from those old *Alien* movies, only in reverse. Anne slumped against me, breathing hard. If there was a rule for this, I didn't know what it was. The only thing I knew was I had to get help.

"I'll be right back. I swear," I said to Anne. "Just...just sit." I helped her onto the floor and then ran down the hall to Dad and Anne's room. The cordless phone was on the nightstand by Anne's side of the bed. I punched in 911. It rang twice.

"9-1-1. What is the nature of your emergency?" asked the voice on the other end.

"My..." I hesitated. What did I call Anne? "My... stepmother. She's pregnant. I think she's in labor. There's blood. But it's way too soon. The baby's not supposed to be born for almost three more months."

"I'm sending an ambulance," the woman said. "Stay on the line. What is your address?"

I gave it to her. "It's the big green house at the top of the street."

"They're on their way."

I swallowed down the sour taste in the back of my throat. "Thank you," I said. There was an old elastic band on the nightstand. It had probably been around yesterday's morning paper. I jammed the phone between my cheek and shoulder and pulled my hair into a ponytail.

"It'll be all right," the woman said. "Now, don't hang up."

"I'm not hanging up." I pulled the quilt off the bed and dragged it down the hall, clutching the phone with my other hand. Anne was sitting with her back to the wall, eyes closed and her legs splayed out in front of her.

"What's your name?" the voice on the other end of the phone asked. "I'm Beth."

"Isabelle." I spread the quilt over Anne and tucked the ends in behind her. "The ambulance is coming," I whispered.

"How old are you, Isabelle?" Beth asked.

"Sixteen."

"Does blood bother you?"

"Um, not really."

"Okay, Isabelle. Don't hang up. Is there something you can cover your stepmother with? It's important to keep her warm."

"I already did."

"Good. Has her water broken?"

I remembered the wet nightgown stuck to the back of Anne's legs. "Yeah, I think so."

"Is she having contractions?"

Before I could answer, Anne grabbed my hand and bit down on her bottom lip so hard tiny spots of blood popped up on it.

"Isabelle? Isabelle, are you still there?"

"I'm here. She just had a contraction."

"The ambulance will be there in just a few more minutes. How far apart are the contractions?"

I wiped the sweat off Anne's face with my sleeve. "I don't know," I said, my voice cracking.

"That's all right," Beth said. "Just tell me as soon as the next one starts."

I felt as though I was edging along a high thin ledge with only Beth's voice to tell me where to set my feet. As long as I listened to her voice I could keep putting one foot in front of the other.

I held on to the phone with one hand and Anne with the other. I concentrated on what Beth was saying until at last the ambulance lights were flashing in the driveway and the paramedics were at the door. I ran down to let them in.

"Up there," I said, pointing up the stairs. "They're here," I said to Beth. My voice cracked again. "Thank you."

"You're welcome, Isabelle," she said before hanging up. "Good luck."

The paramedics—one a man, one a woman—were already bending over Anne. A blood pressure cuff was around one of her arms. Their radios crackled with what sounded like static to me but seemed to make sense to them.

I was useless.

I slipped into my room long enough to pull on jeans and a sweater and grab a pair of shoes and my purse. Then I ran back to Anne and Dad's room and got Anne's wallet out of her purse in case they needed ID or something at the hospital. I didn't let myself think about Dad not being here. I didn't have time to be mad.

The paramedics eased Anne onto a stretcher. I trailed down the steps behind them.

"Isabelle." At the foot of the stairs Anne reached out a hand and I caught it.

"Here."

She grabbed on so tightly I could feel my finger joints snapping. Another contraction. I swallowed hard, pushing down something—I didn't know what.

The guy—his nametag said Dave Florentino—leaned around me. "C'mon, Anne," he coaxed. "Breathe. Breathe."

Anne was almost turned inside out with the pain, pale and sweat-sticky, her bottom lip chewed half raw. And he was telling her to breathe? Like that would fix anything.

I turned my head so I was right in his face. "Do something for her," I said.

He didn't even look at me. "We are," he said.

My free hand clenched into a fist again. I hoped they were. I just couldn't tell.

I climbed into the back of the ambulance behind the stretcher. I wanted Dad, Rafe, even Jason. I wanted someone who'd know what to do. I felt the same overwhelming, longing ache inside for my own mother that I'd felt in the first months after she'd died.

Anne hugged her belly with one arm as though she was trying to protect the baby. I reached over for her other hand. It was the only thing I knew to do. The lights flashed and the siren screamed. And I held on all the way to the hospital.

The emergency room was bright and loud and overflowing with people; arms at weird angles; bloody, swollen mouths; oozing welts; angry purple bruises; faces pinched, gray and frightened. Where had they all come from?

The paramedics wheeled Anne into a small room and I followed. Someone—a nurse—caught my shoulder. "You need to wait outside," she said. I squeezed Anne's hand before I let go. It suddenly looked so much smaller than mine. "I'm just going to be there," I said, pointing to the doorway. "It'll be all right."

She nodded. "Find Marc, please, Isabelle," she whispered.

"I will." Outside the room I grabbed the arm of a guy in pale blue scrubs and streaked green hair. "Excuse me," I said. "Can you tell me where I can find a phone?"

"Sure," he said. "Just go down this hall, around the corner to the left and through the double doors. Phones are at the far end of the waiting room."

Maybe I looked stupid or something because he smiled then and waved me to follow him. I watched for landmarks so I could find my way to Anne again, and wished for a pen so I could draw little arrows on the walls to point the way back.

"Right through here," Spiky said, pointing at a set of doors.

"Thanks," I said.

There were three pay phones. No one was at the middle one. I fished in my purse for change. I had enough for half a dozen phone calls.

Dad's cell phone rang five times. On the sixth ring I heard the stutter that meant the next thing I was going to get was the customer-away-from-the-phone message.

It was the middle of the night. Where was he?

I hung up and my quarter came back. I dialed home and waited for the machine. All I said was, "Dad, I'm with Anne at St. Sebastian's. She needs you."

I stuck another quarter in the slot and remembered Rafe was at a hockey tournament. "Shit!" I laid my forehead against the phone box. Lisa had gone to a concert in Boston with her mother and Sean. Jason. It would have to be Jason.

The phone rang twenty-three times. I counted every ring. Where was Jason's answering machine? Where was Jason at 3:04 in the morning? Where was any of my so-called family?

I saw the nurse who had told me to wait outside head back through the swinging doors. I followed her to Anne's room. A different nurse was checking the IV the paramedics had hooked to Anne's arm. A sloshy, thumping sound filled the room: *whumpa, whumpa, whumpa, whumpa.* The baby's heartbeat? I felt like someone had grabbed me tight around the chest.

"Did you find Marc?" Anne asked as soon as she saw me. A second nurse was wiping her face.

"Not yet," I said as the nurse rubbed a bit of some kind of cream on Anne's chapped lips.

Suddenly Anne closed her eyes and hunched her shoulders. "Oh God," she moaned through her clenched teeth. I caught her hand again without really thinking.

The nurse who had been at the IV moved to another machine, strapped to Anne's belly. It looked like something that might be used to monitor an earthquake. All at once the room filled with people and I ended up shoved back by the door.

I didn't know what they were doing or talking about, but I could tell by how fast it was all happening that something was wrong with the baby. "Where's Isabelle?" I heard Anne ask.

"I'm right here." I pushed my way back to the bed. An orderly had already grabbed the bottom, and a nurse was at the top.

"I'm … bleeding. They have to do a cesarean," she said. The tears in her eyes looked like they'd spill down her face any second.

"That's okay."

"It's too soon," she whispered.

"Lots of babies are born early. It'll be okay. It will." I leaned over and sort of hugged her.

"Let's go," I heard someone say and the bed started moving.

This was not the way it was supposed to be. This was supposed to happen weeks from now. Dad was supposed to be holding Anne's hand and putting cream on her dry lips. Not some nurse. And I should have been with Rafe, eating pizza and kissing sauce off his mouth and complaining about my life.

The nurse who had wiped Anne's face came over to me. "Hi," she said. "Your name's Isabelle?"

I nodded.

"I'm Julie," she said. "Is there someone with you?"

"I'm trying to get my dad." I pushed my hands into my pockets so she wouldn't see them shaking.

She touched my arm, steering me back down the corridor. "Right now you need to go out to the desk and help the unit clerk fill out some papers for your mom."

"Anne is my stepmother," I said stiffly.

"Your stepmother, then. After you're done, tell the clerk you're by yourself and she'll call someone to wait with you until your dad gets here."

"Will the baby be all right?" I asked.

"We'll do our best," Julie said.

"That's not yes." I could feel panic start to rise, like fingers creeping up over the back of my head.

"We'll do everything we can."

What else could she say?

23

I did the best I could with the forms.

"Are you by yourself?" the clerk asked.

"I called my dad," I said. That much wasn't a lie. I didn't want some social worker coming to sit with me. I'd had enough of that after my mom's accident. "He's on his way up. Can you tell me where to go?"

I thought for a second that she was going to ask me more questions. Then a man came through the door with a large nail all the way through the cuff of his denim jacket—and, I was guessing, the arm underneath. At the same time, some skinny, pale guy in the waiting room vomited in his girlfriend's lap. The clerk pointed at the elevator. "Third floor. Follow the signs."

I stopped at the phones and tried Jason again. I tried Dad again. I called the house, punched in the answering machine code and listened to my own message. Nothing.

There was no one in the elevator to the third floor. The hallway was empty as well. I went right, left, then right again and found the waiting room. There wasn't anything else to do but wait.

I sat in a lime Jell-O vinyl chair. There were four *Reader's Digests* and a two-year-old copy of *People* on the table next to the chair. They all had pages missing. I went to the window and looked down at the parking lot. I sat for a while. I walked back to the elevators, where there were two pay phones, and listened to Dad's cell phone give its please-try-again message.

Why didn't he have voice mail on that stupid phone? Why didn't he have it turned on? I closed my eyes and pressed down on the top of my head with my linked hands, as if I could somehow press down my fear.

Maybe I should have let them call a social worker. At least I wouldn't be by myself. Except I didn't want someone to sit with me. I wanted someone who would know what to do. And all at once I knew who that was.

I fished some change out of my pants pocket, dropped it in the slot and pushed the numbers.

24

rs. Mac came down the hall with short, quick steps. Everything got blurry as my eyes filled with tears. She wrapped me in her arms and I laid my cheek against hers. Some of the tears spilled over. I couldn't help it.

Mrs. Mac led me to the sofa under the window. It was the same sticky green vinyl as the chair I'd been sitting in. She pulled a tissue out of her big black purse and handed it to me. I wiped my eyes and took a couple of shaky breaths. "Now blow," she instructed, handing me another one.

I did. Mrs. Mac smiled and tucked the loose piece of hair behind my ear. And then the nurse from down in the emergency room came around the corner. I jumped up. Mrs. Mac stood up as well and her arm went around my shoulders.

"What's going on?" I said.

"I just wanted to check on you," Julie said. "Your stepmother's fine. She'll be settled in a room in a little while. The baby is in the neonatal ICU."

"Wh...wh...what's wrong?" I had trouble shaping the words.

"The baby is very small and her lungs haven't completely developed. She's having some trouble breathing."

A high-pitched whine—a sound like crickets on a summer night—filled my head. "The baby...is she going to die?" I asked.

"We're doing everything we can for her."

"That means you don't know or you don't want to tell me."

"It means we're doing everything we can," Julie said gently.

"Can I at least see her?" I asked.

"Not right now. Someone will let you know when your stepmother is in her room, though."

"Thank you," Mrs. Mac said.

Julie gave her one of those almost-smiles and nodded. Her shoes made soft little squeak-squeaks as she disappeared down the corridor.

I looked down at my hands. I'd picked the right side of my thumbnail raw. "I should try my dad again," I said.

It was the same as all the times before. Suddenly my legs didn't seem to want to walk anymore. They kept sagging on the way back to the waiting room. Mrs. Mac steered me to the sofa. We sat side by side with her arm around me.

"Her name is Leah," I said after a while.

"That's a lovely name," Mrs. Mac said.

And then we waited, my head on her shoulder. There wasn't anything else to do.

"Isabelle?"

I opened my eyes and sat up. Dad, unshaven, in jeans, a sweatshirt and his brown canvas jacket, stood in front of me. Through the window I could see that it was getting light outside. It was morning.

"Where's Anne? What's going on?"

"She had the baby," I said. My voice was thick and raspy. I coughed a couple of times.

"It's too soon," he said, raking a hand through his hair. "What happened? Where are they?" His voice was sharp with anger, like this was somehow my fault.

I felt my own anger rising from somewhere around my stomach up into the back of my throat. "What happened?" I got to my feet and got right in his face. "What happened is Anne was having a baby and no one knew where you were. What happened is she needed you."

I shoved him, both hands flat on his chest. It was like pushing a wall. "You didn't even have your cell phone turned on." I shoved him again. He didn't try to stop me. "You didn't bother telling anyone where you were. Springfield, somewhere. That was helpful. You shouldn't have been there—or anywhere—in the first place." And again. "You suck as a husband and you suck as a father!"

Mrs. Mac caught my arms. "Stop, Isabelle," she said softly. Her tiny hands were surprisingly strong. "Stop. Now." She folded me against her and held on tightly. I was shaking, but there were no tears, only rage.

"I'm Rose McKenzie, Mr. Sullivan," Mrs. Mac said. "Your wife had a cesarean. She should be in a room any time now."

"And the baby?"

"She's very small. They have her in the neonatal ICU." She stroked my hair. "I'm going to take Isabelle home with me for a while. She's exhausted. She took very good care of your wife. You should be proud of her." She said it all without any judgment in her voice.

"I…uh…" Dad hesitated.

He looked like crap. I was glad. Don't touch me, I thought.

"I am," he finally said. He didn't say anything else and neither did I.

25

the air was cool, but the sun was warm when I stepped out of Mrs. Mac's building. She'd made me hot chocolate and toad in the hole—which turned out to be fried egg and bread. I had tried to sleep, but I was full of the kind of jumpy energy you get when you've gone way past tired.

Mrs. Mac must have had a lot of questions, but she didn't ask any. When I left she took my face in both hands for a moment and then kissed my cheek.

"Call me later, dear," she said. "I'll be here all day."

I didn't actually decide to go to Jason's apartment, although my feet turned that way, so some part of me must have. If I'd thought about going over there I would've had to think about why he hadn't answered the phone, and I didn't want to do that.

Rule #48: Be sure your brain is on before your body starts moving.

I climbed up the two flights of stairs to Jason's place and knocked. I didn't bother with the downstairs doorbell because he almost never paid any attention to it. According to Jason, the only people who ever rang his bell were trying to save his soul, and that was a lost cause.

I knocked harder the second time, pounding with the heel of my hand for a long time. Finally I heard someone frigging with the lock on the other side and the door swung open.

Jason was wearing a stretched-out T-shirt that might have been white once. Now, if grunge had a color, this was it. His gray sweatpants had a hole in one knee, and the cuffs were hiked up above his bare, bony ankles.

And he smelled.

"What do you want?" he said.

For a couple of moments I thought I was going to puke on the grubby gold tile in the hallway. Then, just as quickly as it came, the feeling went. I looked at him, dirty and still half buzzed on whatever it was he had used, and I just didn't care anymore. Somewhere inside I'd already known. While the phone had rung twenty-three times unanswered, some part of me had guessed what Jason was doing. I turned and started down the stairs.

"Izzy! Hey, where are you going?" he called. When I didn't stop he came to the top of the stairs. "Iz, c'mon. Stop. I didn't do anything. No pills. Nothing, I swear."

I started counting the steps. *Eight, nine, ten, eleven.*

"I had a few drinks, that's all."

He'd traded drug addict for drunk and that was supposed to be okay. I didn't answer. I just kept counting in my head. *Sixteen, seventeen.*

"You're a self-righteous, prissy little bitch, Izzy," he shouted down the stairwell.

On the bottom step I stopped and looked up at him. "Anne had the baby," I said. Then I pulled open the street door and left.

The hospital was brighter and busier in the daytime. A janitor, mopping the floor by the elevator, told me how to get back to where I'd been the night before. I was headed for the nurses' desk when I spotted Dad, slumped in a chair, in a room halfway down the corridor.

Anne was sleeping, her face pale against green sheets. Dad looked up. Everything sagged on his face and I knew. He glanced at Anne and led me back into the hallway.

"How's Anne?" I asked, keeping my voice low so I wouldn't wake her up. Maybe if I could stop him from actually saying the words it wouldn't be true.

"She'll be all right," he said.

"When can she come home?"

"I don't know." He sighed and his shoulders dropped. "Tomorrow, probably."

I stared at Anne through the half-open door and I could feel Dad looking at me.

"Izzy," he began.

"I'm sorry I went off on you before," I said quickly. I had to keep him from saying it.

"It doesn't matter."

I started talking again, trying to fill up all the empty spaces so he didn't have a chance to speak. "It does matter, and I'm sorry, and—"

"Stop," he said softly. "Just stop for a minute." He put his hands on my shoulders and turned me to face him. I couldn't stop the tears. "She was too small."

I shook my head and twisted out of his grip. I had promised Anne that everything would be all right.

"It was too soon," he whispered. "It was just too soon." I wasn't sure if he was talking to me or to himself.

I closed my eyes and leaned my head against the cold yellow wall. In my mind I could see the fuzzy little baby shape from the ultrasound. Tears spilled down my face. Dad stood beside me, silent, hands jammed in his pockets.

26

Jason showed up at the hospital about an hour and a half later, showered, shaved and phony. I stayed in a chair beside Anne's bed and watched her sleep. It seemed like a better idea than beating him over the head with the stainless steel bedpan from the nightstand.

Anne came home from the hospital the next afternoon. She moved slowly and stiffly, as though every step hurt. I didn't know how to say what I needed to say. "I'm sorry" was all that finally came out.

"It wasn't your fault," Anne said. She looked empty. All the emotion was gone from her face and her voice. "Thank you for everything you did."

"If I can do anything for you, please just ask, okay," I said. She nodded.

I watched her make her way up the stairs, one at a time. Jason didn't show up at the house for another day.

I was at the kitchen counter making cinnamon toast and tea for Anne. All the hairs went up on the back of my neck—

some kind of prehistoric early-warning system kicking in—
before he even spoke.

"Hey, Izzy. What're you doing?" he said.

"I'm making a tray for Anne."

I didn't turn around. I cut two slices of bread, dropped
them in the toaster, brushed the crumbs into the sink and
rooted in the cupboard for the cinnamon sugar. In my mind
I saw myself grinding the rest of the loaf into Jason's lying,
drunk's face. I was breathing hard, as though I'd been running
from something.

"How is she?" he asked finally.

"About how you'd think she'd be."

"You okay?"

I set down the knife I was holding and swung around.
"Anne's not okay. Dad's not okay. I'm not okay. Why don't
you ask me what you really want to know, Jason? Did I rat
you out?"

"I had a couple of drinks," he said with that I-haven't-
done-anything-wrong tone I remembered from when he
used to scarf whatever pills he could get his hands on. I
noticed he'd shaved and gotten his hair cut. His clothes were
clean—no holes. Someone had ironed his shirt. It was all part
of a big put-on. I remembered that, too.

"Yeah, right," I said. "How big was the glass?"

"Oooh, good one, Iz," he said, smirking. "Tell me something,
do you ever have fun? Or are you always Little Miss Perfect?"

"Let me see, drug addict, drunk, liar." I made a show
of counting on my fingers. "Are you always a total freaking screwup?"

He closed his eyes for a moment and shook his head. "Heard it, heard it, heard it, Isabelle. For once, stay out of my life."

I looked at him, sprawled in the chair, and I realized that I didn't want to clean up his puke anymore. I didn't want to listen to his excuses or make excuses for him. I didn't want to be around Jason. I didn't like him. I wasn't sure I could even love him anymore.

"I am out of your life. Things are bad enough here, Jason. I didn't say anything. And I won't."

The toast popped then and the water was boiling in the kettle. I made the tea, buttered the bread and arranged things on the tray.

"What do you want me to do?" Jason asked then. His tone had gone from pissed to whiney.

"I don't care what you do," I said. I just sounded tired. "Leave me out of it."

I picked up the tray and moved past him. It wasn't my job to look after Jason. Besides, I hadn't managed to save him the last time. I couldn't save anyone. I could barely take care of myself these days.

27

t he funeral was on Thursday. It was nothing like the memo-
rial service for my mother. That day there were too many
flowers, too many people, too many fake smiles.

This was just the opposite: just Anne, Dad, Jason and me,
along with Anne's minister friend. And a tiny brass urn that
seemed way too small. Anne stood silent and stiff next to a
hole in the ground draped with too-green fake grass. Her skin
was so pale even the wind didn't bring color to her cheeks.

I stood to her left, back a little, clutching three yellow dai-
sies. It was as far away as I could get from that brass container. I listened to the minister talk about eternal life and I laid
my flowers next to the others when it was time.

The sky was a deep, endless blue and the sun was warm on
the back of my head. It felt wrong. The sky should have been
full of dark, heavy clouds. It should have been raining.

Dad, Anne and I drove home in silence. Jason had said
he would walk. Maybe he was going off to get drunk. I
didn't care.

Life went on, sort of. We were walking, talking, breathing, Dad and Anne and I, but we were like those mannequins you see in a department store window: there was nothing inside. Rafe's mother filled the refrigerator with food nobody ate.

I hadn't cried since the hospital. Whenever Rafe put his arms around me I pressed against him, hoping that somehow I could fill myself with his warmth. "What can I do?" he'd ask. I didn't have an answer.

Every few days Mrs. Mac called to check on me. The conversation always ended the same way. "If you need anything, please call me," she'd say. I always promised I would.

In class I was on autopilot. I studied notes I didn't remember taking and handed in assignments I didn't remember doing. Sometimes I caught Lisa watching me. I knew she was worried about me, but I didn't know what to say to her.

I started taking long, roundabout routes home from school, mindlessly putting one foot in front of the other. One afternoon I passed Keyes Deli. A man was at the counter in the window eating noodle soup, and I stopped on the sidewalk, remembering the first time Anne had made soup for us.

That night I took Anne's cookbook, the one that had belonged to her grandmother, down from the cupboard over the sink. The next day after school I took the shortest way home. I stopped at the grocery store and carried out two plastic sacks of supplies.

The soup smelled wonderful and tasted almost as good. I filled a bowl and arranged some little fish-shaped crackers on a plate.

Anne was in the living room, curled in the wing chair, staring out the window. "I brought you something to eat," I said.

She turned her head. "Thank you, Isabelle," she said.

I set the tray on the table to her left. She looked over at it and then turned back to the window.

When I went back to get the tray about half an hour later, she hadn't even picked up the spoon. I started back to the kitchen.

"Isabelle?"

I stopped and turned partway around. Curled into the chair, Anne looked swamped in her sweatshirt, as though it were a couple of sizes too big. It probably was. She hardly ever ate.

She gestured at the tray. "Thank you," she said. "I'm just not hungry right now."

"It's okay," I said. "Maybe I can get you something later."

"Maybe."

I went into the kitchen and set the tray on the counter by the sink. I was just so sorry. But I didn't know how to say it so Anne could hear me.

I was sitting at the table with my own bowl when Dad came in. "Where's Anne?" he asked.

"I think she went for a walk," I said. I'd heard her go out about ten minutes before.

His shoulders sagged and he let his breath out slowly.

He hadn't shaved, I noticed. And he needed a haircut. It was like he was sleepwalking most of the time, like he wasn't aware of what was happening. I couldn't help wondering if he and Anne would make it through this. Once he had asked,

"Are you all right?" And I'd said, "Yes," even though I wasn't. We pretty much avoided each other, and when we couldn't, we slipped past one another and didn't make eye contact.

"I'll be in the office," Dad said finally.

I nodded. A part of me felt sorry for him—the baby was his too. But a part of me hated him for starting it all. I didn't want to hate my own father, but I had to walk a wide circle around him because otherwise I might start screaming, and I wasn't sure if I'd be able to stop.

18

"Do you know where Jason is?" Dad asked.

I knew by the tightness of his jaw and the way the words squeezed out of his mouth that he was upset. "No," I said, shaking my head as I spread peanut butter all the way out to the edge of a piece of toast. "It's Friday night. He's probably downtown outside the liquor store doing old sixties songs." Or inside looking for something to drink, I added silently.

"He said he had a job."

"Jason thinks singing in front of the liquor store for change is a job." I took a big bite of toast so I wouldn't have to talk about Jason anymore.

Dad rubbed the back of his neck. His hair was down over the collar of his shirt. Was he ever going to get it cut?

"I loaned him the truck to move some equipment. He was supposed to have it back here by six."

I sucked in a breath in the middle of swallowing and almost choked. I started to cough, spraying toast crumbs all over the counter.

"You all right?" Dad asked.

I waved him away. "Sorry," I gasped. "It went down the wrong hole."

It was ten after seven by the clock over the refrigerator. Was Jason stupid enough to drive when he was drinking? Maybe. He was stupid enough to be drinking in the first place.

I knew this was where I was supposed to tell Dad about finding Jason drunk. And if he'd been the old Dad and I'd been the old Isabelle, that's what would have happened. Instead I mumbled and shrugged and escaped upstairs to my room.

But I couldn't stay still. All the questions I had about Jason—Where was he? Was he drunk? Had he had an accident?—were jumping around in my mind. I looked out into the hallway. The cordless phone was lying on the table at the top of the stairs. I darted out and snagged it.

Rafe picked up on the third ring. I could hear him smile when he knew it was me. "Can you pick me up now?" I asked. "There's something I have to do. I'll explain when I see you."

"Sure. I'll be there in fifteen minutes."

"No, no. Pick me up at the end of the street. At the corner."

"What for?"

"Because I asked you to."

For once I was glad that Rafe wasn't like anyone else's boyfriend. He didn't say, "Are you crazy?" or "Is it that time of the month?" He just said, "Okay."

I pulled my blue polar fleece sweatshirt with the hood and the kangaroo pocket over my head. It took a couple of minutes, but I managed to find a pair of gloves that matched each other and a red knit beanie hat on the floor of my closet.

Dad was on the phone downstairs. I gave him a quick wave and escaped out the door. I hadn't wanted to stand around waiting for Rafe because I didn't want to have to lie to Dad about where I was going. I didn't want to talk to him until I knew what was going on with Jason. I waited at the corner, shifting from one foot to the other and watching the cars for Rafe.

"So where are we going?" he asked after he'd kissed me and I'd buckled my seat belt.

"Jason's apartment."

We drove for maybe a minute in silence. Then Rafe spoke. "You gonna tell me why I had to pick you up at the corner?"

"I don't want anyone to know where I'm going." I pulled at a piece of dry skin on my bottom lip. "It just seemed easier."

"Why?"

"Look, you can't tell anyone."

"That'll be easy," Rafe said, glancing over at me for a second. "Because I don't know anything."

The only way to say it was all at once. "Jason borrowed Dad's truck, but he didn't bring it back and he's not answering the phone and the thing is, he's been drinking—getting drunk—and—" I let out the breath I didn't even realize I'd been holding. "And maybe…and maybe other stuff. I don't know."

I waited.

Rafe kept his eyes on the road. "I thought you weren't going to do this anymore," he said finally.

"What do you mean? Do what?"

"Cover for Jason."

"I'm not covering for Jason," I said.

Rafe didn't say anything.

"I'm not," I insisted, twisting in my seat so I could see more of his face. "This is different. How could I tell Dad? It was when Anne…I went over to Jason's apartment and he was drunk. Dirty, gross, drunk. And then when I got to the hospital…" I laced my fingers tightly together "…Dad told me…about the baby."

I looked out the window. We were at a red light. "What was I supposed to do, Rafe?" I whispered. "Say, 'Hey, Dad. Jason's drunk'? How could I do that?" I pressed my laced fingers against my mouth and took a couple of shaky breaths.

I knew by how stiff Rafe was that he was pissed at me. "So why didn't you tell me?" he said.

The light changed.

I opened my mouth, but at first nothing came out. "I couldn't ask you to lie for Jason," I said finally. "I'm sorry. I was just trying to do the right thing for everyone. Now it's worse."

We drove a block in silence. Then Rafe laid his right hand, palm up, on the seat between us. I put my hand on top of his and he folded his fingers around mine.

We parked in front of Jason's building. The truck wasn't on the street. I jabbed the doorbell with my thumb as we passed it.

Upstairs I pounded on Jason's door, the same way I had the morning I'd found him drunk. Nothing. Rafe reached over my shoulder and beat on the door with his flat hand. But there was no sound from inside.

Slowly, silently, I counted to twenty. In my head I saw Jason, stoned, sitting on the kitchen counter, talking so fast the words didn't make sense. I saw him sprawled on the bathroom floor, head against the upturned toilet seat, flecks of puke on his T-shirt. I saw him straddling the top crossbar of the swing set in the same park my mom had taken us to when we were little, swinging his legs as he sang "I'm a Little Teapot".

I tried the doorknob. It turned. I pushed, and the door swung open a couple of inches.

Rafe's arm snaked around my shoulders. "I'll see if he's in there," he said.

I shook my head, reached up and clutched the hand on my shoulder. Then I nudged the door open the rest of the way with my foot.

We both gagged at the smell, a mix of BO and garbage that hadn't been taken out for days. I felt along the wall for the light switch.

"Holy shit," Rafe said when the light came on.

The only piece of furniture was a peeling brown vinyl recliner in the middle of the living room. A grubby blue blanket was wadded up on the seat. There were five beer bottles standing on the floor next to the chair and a bigger bottle of something else—vodka, maybe—lying empty on its side.

The sofa was gone, and the big wooden cupboard Dad had built that Jason used for his TV and stereo. Where was his sound system, his keyboard, the answering machine? My mother's rocking chair. Where was Mom's rocking chair?

I stood there cold and numb while Rafe scouted around.

"Jason's not here," he said, reaching for my hand. "And this is it for the furniture. C'mon. Let's go." I let him lead me back down the stairs.

Outside I looked up and down the street again; still no sign of the truck. "Can we just go down the alley and see if the truck's maybe in the back somewhere?" I asked.

Rafe shrugged. "Sure."

"Be there. Be there. Be there. Be there," I repeated under my breath.

Jason had knocked over two garbage cans when he parked, but the truck was there, next to the building's fire escape. My knees went wobbly with relief. Rafe slowly circled the truck, looking for damage.

"It looks okay as far as I can tell," he said. "What do you want to do?"

"I want to beat on my dumb-ass brother with something really hard," I said. "Maybe one of those big hammers that construction workers use to tear down walls." I folded my arms across my chest and tucked my icy fingers into my armpits for warmth. "I hate him, Rafe," I said. "He uses everyone. He uses me like I'm some kind of cash machine. He doesn't care about me. The only person he cares about is himself. And I should just—" I stopped, swallowed hard as tears filled my eyes.

I looked past Rafe, out toward the street, half expecting Jason to come swaggering up the alley. "I know it doesn't make sense. Why do I care about what's happened to him? He wouldn't if it were me. It's just...I can't stop thinking, what if he's had an accident? What if he passed out somewhere and choked on his own barf? I can't...I have to do something."

I was shaking. Rafe pulled me into a hug. "The truck's here, so we know he's not driving," he said. He paused. "I'd like to pound his head on the back bumper about ten times." He made a growling noise in the back of his throat. "Your brother's an asshole, Iz. You gotta go home and tell your dad what's going on."

"I know," I whispered. And I would have done anything to get out of it.

29

I stood in the driveway, thinking I might heave my toast and peanut butter under the Chinese gooseberry. I'd convinced Rafe to go drive around downtown and look for Jason while I talked to Dad. I guess I was holding out hope that somehow this would be a mistake instead of another one of Jason's screwups.

"Just tell him," Rafe had said. "Do it fast, like pulling off a bandage."

Why did people always say that? As if doing something quicker was easier, as if it didn't still hurt.

I went in, peeling off my gloves and hat. Dad was in the living room with the phone stuck to his ear. I stood in the doorway, wiping my sweaty hands on my jeans. My feet wouldn't go any farther. Dad pushed the disconnect button. "Where in hell are you?" he muttered, dropping the handset on the table. He turned and caught sight of me. "Hi, what did you forget?"

For a second I wasn't sure the words would come out. But they did. "I think Jason's in trouble," I said, almost choking on his name.

"You got that right," Dad said, doing the hand-hair thing again.

"No, Dad. I mean … Jason's … drinking."

He froze for a moment. His hand slid over the back of his head in slow motion and hung on his neck for a moment. "What do you mean, Jason's drinking?"

"When Anne … the baby … he was, he was drunk when I went over there in the morning." I couldn't seem to stop rubbing my hands on my pants. I jammed them in my pockets.

"And you're just telling me about this now?" He was across the room, in front of me, in a flash. "He's an addict. For God's sake, Izzy, use your brain. Jason could be out there right now, driving around drunk. He could kill someone. He could kill himself." With each word he got louder.

"No, no he's not. The truck's behind his apartment and, and it's okay, I swear."

"How do you—" He stopped. A tiny muscle twitched at the corner of his left eye. "Is that where you were?"

"Yes." Something sour and acidic burned at the back of my throat.

"Is Jason there?"

I shook my head.

"How do I know you're telling the truth?"

"I am. The apartment was empty."

"You've been lying for weeks, but now you've decided to tell the truth."

"I wasn't lying." My own voice was getting louder. "I didn't tell you Jason was drinking. That's not the same as lying."

"Oh, c'mon. He's a drug addict and now it turns out he's

a drunk, too. And you just keep covering for him." Dad was right in my face now.

I took a couple of steps backward.

"Don't walk away from me," he warned, his voice hoarse with anger. "What's the matter with you? Don't you remember what it was like at the hospital the last time with Jason? Tubes jammed up his nose and down his throat and in his arms. He looked like the bones would rip through his skin, he was so thin. You want to put us through that again?" He grabbed both my arms and I didn't know if he was going to shake me or drag me into the living room.

"Marc, stop."

We both turned. Anne was on the second step from the bottom of the staircase. I hadn't heard her come down.

Dad loosened his grip on me. I yanked away from him and took another step back.

"Jason's drinking," Dad said. His voice was cold.

Anne nodded. "I know. I heard." She looked tired. There were puffy pouches under both her eyes.

"And Izzy's been covering for him."

My own anger finally spilled over. "What should I have done, Dad?" I shouted. "Come back to the hospital and say, 'Jason's drunk and he smells like a sewer'? Yeah, I remember what it was like with Jason at the hospital the last time. Don't you remember what it was like for all of us at the hospital *this* time?"

He looked away from me.

"I thought you had enough hurt to carry around. And I figured when things got better I'd tell you." I looked up at the ceiling for a moment and swallowed a couple of times so I wouldn't start crying. "But they didn't."

The silence hung like a haze in the room.

"I'm all through," Dad said at last, still not looking at me. "I don't care what Jason does. I don't care what he drinks, what he takes, what he shoves up his nose or in his arm. I'm done."

"No! We have to find him. Dad. All of his stuff—it's gone. The CD player, his keyboard—the furniture."

Anne shook her head. "Don't do this, Marc," she said.

"I. Don't. Care." He said each word slowly, carefully, as though he was speaking a different language. Finally he looked at me. There was nothing in his face. No anger. No hurt. No sadness.

I turned away, pulling on my hat.

"Where are you going?" Dad asked.

This time I didn't look at him. "To find Jason," I said.

His hand snapped out like a snake striking. He grabbed my right arm just below the shoulder. "No, you're not."

I tried to pull back and twist out of his grip, but he held on tightly. "Let go!" I shouted.

"No!" He gave me a little shake. His face had gone white with fury except for two red blotches, one on each cheek.

"I have to find Jason," I shouted. I was half crying and trying to catch my breath. "He's in trouble. Let me go!"

Anne stepped between us then. She put her hands on Dad's chest. "Let go of her, Marc," she said. "Now." Her voice grew more insistent. "Let go." She kept her face in front of his so he had to look at her, and in a moment he dropped his hand. I could still feel his fingers on my arm.

"Jesus, Anne," he said, almost whispering the words. "What am I supposed to do? Jason's a freaking screwup. How many times am I supposed to bail him out? How many chances is he supposed to get?"

"I don't know," Anne said, her hands sliding off his chest.

I pulled on my gloves and moved toward the door. "I'm going," I said.

Anne studied Dad's face. Then she let out a breath and turned to me. "Isabelle. Wait." She took three steps past me and grabbed her big duffle coat from a hanger in the closet.

Dad swung back around to face us. "Anne, what the hell are you doing?"

She buttoned the jacket and checked both pockets before she looked at him. "Look what losing our baby has done to us, Marc," she said. "What will losing Jason do?"

"Rescuing Jason won't make up for losing . . . for what happened."

She pressed her lips together and I knew she was trying not to cry. "Maybe. But I don't want to bury another child." She turned to me and straightened her shoulders. Her eyes were very bright. "Let's go," she said.

I opened the door and stepped outside, keeping my eyes on Anne and not once looking back.

30

I shivered. It seemed a lot colder than it had been earlier.

Rafe was parked across the street. He got out of the car and crossed to us.

"Did you find him?" I asked, even though I knew the answer was no. If Rafe had found Jason, Jason would've been here, even if Rafe had to throw Jason in the back and tie him down with the seat belt.

Rafe shook his head. "You talk to your dad?" he asked, his eyes flicking over to Anne for a second.

All I could do was nod.

"So now what?"

"We need to find Jason," Anne said, pulling a hat and gloves out of her coat pocket.

Rafe turned to face her. "He's not in front of the liquor store and no one there's seen him today. I checked the alley and even the dumpsters. I went back to the apartment and checked all around there, too."

"Isabelle, is there anywhere Jason might go?" Anne asked.

I had to think for a minute, hunched up against the cold with my fingers pulled into my sleeves for warmth. "The diner maybe," I said finally. "He used to spend a lot of time in the music room at the library. And there was this club—I can't remember the name, but it's at the bottom of Alexander Street—he plays there sometimes. At least I think he still does." It struck me that I knew very little about Jason's life anymore. That I hadn't wanted to.

"Let's start at the library," Anne said. "It's the closest."

"I can drive," Rafe said.

"Thanks." Anne gave him what passed for a smile.

Rafe put his arm around my shoulders and pulled me against him as we headed for the car. It was like being wrapped in a warm blanket. "You gonna tell me what's going on?" he asked in a low voice.

"Later," I said. "What if we can't find Jason?" I asked Anne.

"We haven't even looked yet."

"What if he's …?" I couldn't finish the sentence.

Anne touched my arm and it seemed as though I could feel the warmth of her hand through my coat and her glove. "Let's just look, okay?" she said.

"Okay."

As Rafe pulled away from the curb I couldn't help looking back over my shoulder at the house. I didn't really know what I hoped to see—the twitch of a curtain maybe, something to show that Dad was watching. But nothing moved.

Jason wasn't at the library. Anne checked the music room while Rafe and I searched the stacks on both floors. I remembered that when Jason used to get stoned, sometimes he'd sleep in the upstairs reading alcoves. When I turned the corner at the end of a long shelf of books and saw a pair of knobby-soled black boots sticking into the aisle, I felt a rush of exhilaration. At the same time my legs went all soft, like I was held together by a Slinky instead of bones.

It wasn't Jason. It was a guy about the same age with his tongue stuck in the mouth of the girl on his lap. I had the urge to kick his feet and knock them both to the floor. I caught my foot starting to move and quickly stepped over his outstretched legs, mumbling "excuse me" as I went by.

There were maybe a dozen people at the diner. And none of them were Jason. "I'll check the can," Rafe said. "You never know."

Anne was at the counter by the cash register. "I'm going to get coffee," she said. "Would you like hot chocolate?"

"Okay," I said without looking around. I was watching the sidewalk through the plate-glass window, hoping somehow that Jason would come sauntering past.

"What about Rafe?" Anne asked, just as he came from the back of the restaurant shaking his head.

I turned away from the window then. "Oh, uh, coffee for him. Two cream, two sugar."

We sat in the car, hands warming around our cardboard cups. "You said there's a place Jason used to play," Anne said, leaning forward with her elbows up on the back of the front seat.

"Yeah," I said. "I can't remember the name of the place, but I think I could find it."

"Good. What about his friends?"

"I, uh … don't know." I could feel my face getting hot. "I mean, I just know the people he used to get wrecked with. I don't know who he hangs out with now."

"What about the guys he was in the band with?" Rafe said. "Maybe he's back hanging out with them."

"Good idea," Anne said.

"Uh, let me see," I said. "Kevin Meldrum, Shane Roberts and … Michael … Michael … Michael Clark." Anne's cell phone rang then. I jerked at the sound, slopping hot chocolate onto the back of my hand.

Anne reached into her pocket and slowly pulled out the phone. She looked down at it and shot a quick glance at the car window. I licked hot chocolate off my hand and wondered if she was going to roll down the window and chuck the phone out onto the sidewalk.

But that wasn't the kind of thing Anne did. Then it occurred to me that maybe it was. I didn't know much about Jason and his life. What did I know about Anne?

"Hello," she said. In a second her head came up and she looked at me. "We're both fine," she said.

Dad.

"That's a very good idea … No … I think you should do what you're doing … Not now, Marc. Let's concentrate on finding Jason … All right. I'll call you in a little while. Bye." She disconnected and put the phone back in her pocket. Her eyes were still locked on my face. "Your father's been calling the guys Jason used to … spend time with."

I studied a tiny cut in the web of skin between my thumb

and first finger. I didn't trust my voice to work. I felt Rafe's hand touch my knee. "That's good," I finally said.

Anne cleared her throat and I looked up then. The smile she gave me was almost a real one. "Let's see if we can find that club," she said.

I spotted the building the second time Rafe cruised along the narrow street. We waited in the car while Anne went inside and then came out less than fifteen minutes later. She shook her head as she headed back toward us.

"Now what?" Rafe said as Anne slid into the back.

I slumped against the seat, squeezing the top of my head between my hands, half hoping an answer would pop out. "I don't know," I said. "I feel like we're looking in the wrong places."

"Why?" Anne asked.

"Well, before, I mean when Jason was getting stoned all the time, it wasn't a social thing for him." I twisted in the seat so I could look at both Anne and Rafe at the same time.

"You're right," Rafe said. "He was always off by himself."

I nodded. "And every time he got found out he got sneakier. He never stopped trying to hide what he was doing. It was like if he was hiding it, it wasn't really a problem."

"So you think that's what he's doing this time?" Anne said.

"Yeah…maybe. The only reason I found out Jason was drinking was because he never expected me to just show up at his door like that."

"Do you remember where he used to go?" Anne asked, hunching into her coat as though she were cold.

"Mostly didn't he just stay in his apartment?" Rafe said.

"Uh-huh. Not the one he has now, though."

My head was too hot. I pulled off my hat and took my hair out of its ponytail. *Where are you, Jason?* I asked in my head. I closed my eyes and made myself think back to what it was like before Jason went to rehab. It wasn't somewhere I liked to go. Pictures flashed into my mind, images of Jason one after another as though someone was clicking the shutter of a camera too fast.

"Butternut Square," I said slowly.

"Excuse me," Anne said.

"You mean that little park over where the old hospital used to be?" Rafe asked.

"Sometimes Jason goes there." I opened my eyes. "At least, he did. Before. It's really small. Not a lot of people even know about it. We used to go…we played there when we were kids."

I'd almost said the park was where my mom used to take us. It didn't seem right to talk about my mother in front of Anne right then. When Mom first died I'd go and sit in the park all the time. It was one of her favorite places and it seemed that if anything was left of her, that would be where I'd find it. Later, when it got harder to hold on to her, I'd sit on a bench under one of the big beechnut trees and it was as if all my memories went from being foggy to bright, from just out of focus to sharp and clear.

"I think it's worth a look," Anne said, pressing her hands against the small of her back to stretch. She looked at Rafe. "You know how to get there?"

"Not a problem."

Anne touched my shoulder. "We will find him. I promise."

I nodded silently. I remembered promising her that the baby would be all right. It wasn't the kind of promise you could keep.

31

In the orange-pink glow from the streetlights the park looked like something out of a bad horror movie. The damp air had collected in clumps of fog that half covered everything at ground level.

The park sat on the hill, boxed by four streets into a long rectangle. The swings and teeter-totters were at the bottom. A statue of the poet Robert Burns, green with copper tarnish, loomed over a concrete fountain near the top. There were benches stuck all around.

Rafe parked at the bottom of the hill under an elm tree with long, peeling bark and we all got out of the car. I felt like fanning away the puffs of fog so I could see better.

I moved away from Anne and Rafe, leaving them to check the swings and the rest of the kiddie stuff. I looked behind a bench and underneath it, walked slowly around a huge tree. Working my way toward the fountain, my insides lurched every time I saw a dark lump on the ground and then sank when it turned out to be a dirty mound of snow or a ragged bush.

"Jason, where are you?" I whispered, stepping over a garbage bag partly frozen to the ground. In the fog it had looked like the sleeve of a shirt.

I came around the edge of the fountain and almost fell over Jason, lying on the concrete, his head and one arm on the lip of the water pool. "Oh God," someone moaned. Me? I dropped to my knees beside him. My hand was shaking so hard I could barely get it to his face. His skin was clammy and very, very cold.

"Rafe! Anne!" I screamed, pulling off my sweatshirt, fighting with the sticky zipper at the neck. It came loose and I tucked it around Jason. All he had on was a long-sleeved T-shirt and jeans.

"Aw, shit," Rafe said behind me.

I looked up at him. "He's so cold," I said.

"Lemme see." Rafe bent over Jason.

"Oh, Lord, no." Anne. She dropped to her knees next to Rafe. I sat back on my heels, hugging myself and shivering.

Rafe felt along Jason's neck and nodded at Anne. Then he leaned close to Jason's face and immediately reared back. "Whoa! What's he been drinking?"

Anne already had her cell phone out. "Where are we exactly?" she asked Rafe, pushing 9-1-1.

"Top of the square. That's Duke Street," he said, pointing just beyond the fountain. Anne turned her body away from us and spoke to the 911 operator.

Rafe looked at me then. "He's breathing. I think he might've hit his head. I don't want to move him to check, though."

Bits of gravel were stuck to a raw, oozing scrape on Jason's cheek. I fumbled in the pocket of my jacket, trying to keep it over him, and finally pulled out a Kleenex. I wiped at the dirt, working at keeping my hand steady and not hurting Jason.

"The ambulance is on the way," Anne said. She looked at me as though she'd only just noticed I was there. "Isabelle, you're freezing." She started undoing her coat.

"No." Rafe held up one hand. He already had his own jacket half off. He pulled out his other arm and handed the jacket over to me. "Here, Izzy. Put this on," he said.

I hesitated.

"You want to get hypothermia?"

I took the jacket and glanced down at Jason.

"Jason has enough antifreeze in his system," Rafe said, as though he'd read my thoughts. "C'mon. Put it on before you freeze."

The warmth of Rafe's body still clung to the material. I hugged my shoulder and breathed in his scent from the sleeve. In the distance a siren whined.

I bent over Jason again. "C'mon, Jason, wake up," I whispered. But he didn't.

"I'll go stand at the corner and wait for the ambulance," Rafe announced, getting to his feet.

"Thank you," Anne said.

I just nodded. The lump in my throat had gotten so big I wasn't sure I could talk. Rafe laid his hand on my hair for a second as he moved past me.

I bent forward and kissed Jason's forehead. He smelled of sweat, filth and vomit. "Don't die, you big puke," I whispered.

One of Jason's hands was sticking out from under the edge of my sweatshirt. The skin was scraped off two knuckles and the fingers were icy and limp. I laced my own through them and held on for both of us.

32

Rafe drove with one hand and I held on to the other one, as though it were a rope, all the way to the hospital. If something bad was going to happen, it would. It didn't matter what I did. I didn't have the power to control that.

The ambulance raced up the driveway, under the breezeway and around to the side of the emergency room. Rafe stopped in the no-parking zone by the front doors. I pulled at my seat belt. The latch wouldn't let go. He leaned over, undid the buckle and kissed me, catching only the corner of my mouth.

"I'll park and I'll be right there," he said. "It'll be okay."

I didn't bother to tell him how lame those words were. The emergency room doors opened with a swoosh. I followed Anne. That choking lump was back in my throat and I couldn't swallow it down.

Dad was standing at the registration desk. Anne must have called him, I realized. His face was ashy and I didn't remember all those lines around his mouth. He still cared about Jason. It didn't matter what he'd said before.

Dad wiped one hand across his face. "I should've seen this."

"Don't," Anne said. She laid her hand against his cheek for a moment. "What matters is we found him."

"Mr. Sullivan?" The speaker, a nurse I guessed, wore a lavender uniform and a jacket covered with bears in feather boas doing the cancan. "If you come with me you can see your son."

"Go," Anne said. "We'll wait over there."

"Are you okay?" he asked. "Being here?"

"I'm fine. Go."

"Izzy, are you all right?" Dad said.

I hadn't been sure he'd even noticed me. "Yeah, I am," I said. I sounded as though I was getting a cold. "Go see Jason."

"I'll be back as soon as I can."

His hands were all over the place, the way they'd been the day of the wedding and the morning we'd stood in the hallway outside Anne's room and he'd told me about the baby. Why had it taken until now for me to notice that my father's hands went spastic when he was afraid?

Anne and I turned toward the waiting room. Rafe was just coming in. I left Anne and walked over to him. "Why don't you go home?" I said. "We're just going to wait."

"Not likely," Rafe said, resting one arm across my shoulder. "So don't even try to get rid of me."

The ER had two waiting rooms, big spaces on either side of the registration desk. The left side seemed to be the quiet room. We found three chairs by the windows. I could hear a TV in the other waiting room, loud enough to be annoying but not so loud that I could get enough words to figure out what was on.

"How about a coffee?" Rafe said to Anne.

She slid both hands over her forehead and through her hair. With her bangs pulled off her face she looked like a teenager. "Umm, yes, Rafe," she said. "That would be good." She reached for her coat.

Rafe waved a hand in the air. "Hey, no. I'll get it."

"All right. Thanks." Anne leaned back and let out a slow breath.

"Hot chocolate, Iz?" Rafe said to me.

"Yeah." I pulled off his jacket and pushed it against the chair back.

"I'll be back," he said, his hand brushing my arm on the way by.

I leaned my head back until it touched the window and closed my eyes. I wanted to pray but I couldn't think of any prayers other than "Now I lay me down to sleep." I settled for silently asking God to take care of Jason. No one else had been able to do it—not even Jason himself.

Anne and I sat there without talking for what seemed like a long time, although it couldn't have been. "Jason will be all right," Anne said suddenly.

"You don't know that," I said without moving or even opening my eyes.

"This isn't your fault."

"It is. I should have told Dad that Jason was drinking."

"Uh-huh. You should have."

I opened my eyes and turned my head to look at her. That wasn't what she was supposed to say.

"You should have said something." The front of Anne's hair was still sticking up. "I know you didn't because ..." She stopped and swallowed. "We were all so ... hurt. I understand why you didn't want to make things any worse. But even if you had told someone, it doesn't mean we wouldn't still be sitting here. You don't know if Jason would've stopped drinking."

"And you don't know that he wouldn't have," I said.

Anne propped an elbow on the armrest and leaned her head on her hand. "That's right. I don't know and you don't know." She sighed. "You can't control what other people do, Isabelle."

I stared at the ceiling—even rows of pebbly rectangular tiles. "I didn't do anything. I didn't even try to help him."

"You can't stop Jason drinking. That's up to him."

"I know but—"

"You can't always make things work out the way you want them to. You tried pretty hard to stop your father from marrying me, but you couldn't." Her mouth moved, but for a moment no words came out. "You did everything, everything, for me and for ... the baby and you couldn't ..."

She didn't have to finish the sentence. My eyes began to burn. I pressed one fist against my mouth.

"Horrible things happen, Isabelle. You can't always stop them. No matter how much you want to."

"I don't want him to die." My hand was trembling even though my fingers were clenched so tightly the blood had drained away from the skin on the knuckles. All of me was shaking. "I told him I didn't care what he did and I thought I meant it…but I didn't."

This time I couldn't stop the tears from spilling over. Anne put both arms around me. I was rigid, tears flooding my face. Anne let go with one arm long enough to fish a Kleenex out of her pocket. I wiped my face and took a couple of deep, shuddering breaths.

"You were the one who knew where to find Jason," Anne said. "You might have saved his life. Think about that."

I sat up. My eyes felt swollen and scratchy. I rubbed them but that just made it worse.

"Why don't you go splash some water on your face?" Anne said, pointing. "There's a bathroom over there."

I hesitated.

"If anything happens I'll come get you."

The washroom walls were neon yellow. The buzzing fluorescent light over the sink gave off a pinky-yellow glow. The combination made me look like I had jaundice—or maybe the plague.

I filled the basin with cold water and splashed it on my face until my cheeks were tingling. I dried off with scratchy brown paper towels and fixed my ponytail.

Anne looked small and scared sitting by herself in the waiting room. But she was stronger than she looked. **If it looks like a duck and it quacks like a duck, it's a duck—or a chicken with a good acting coach. Rule #…** I couldn't remember.

"Better?" Anne asked.

I nodded. My top lip seemed to suddenly be stuck to my teeth. "I…uh…" The words I wanted to say felt like they were stuck too. "If you hadn't got me thinking about where Jason hung out I might not have remembered about the park." The rest of it came out in a rush. "You're the one who saved Jason."

I almost hugged her. I could feel myself starting to move toward her. No one would have been able to see it, but I could feel it.

Then out of the corner of my eye I saw Rafe stopped at the far end of the waiting room, by the breezeway, balancing three cardboard cups and looking everywhere but at Anne and me. I took a step back. "There's Rafe," I said. "I'll just go…help…him."

"Go ahead," Anne said. She shooed me away with one hand.

I walked over to Rafe and took the top container off the stack.

"That's coffee," he said. "Bottom one's yours."

We switched cups.

"You want me to go and…go?" he asked.

I tucked a stray bit of hair behind my ear. "It's all right. Anne and I are okay."

He studied my face as though he could tell by looking whether or not I was lying. I touched his arm and made myself smile at him. "Really," I said. "It's okay."

We walked back to Anne. "Thank you, Rafe," she said, taking the cup he handed her and standing up. "I'm going to see what I can find out about Jason."

"Okay," I said.

Anne hesitated. One hand moved as though maybe she was going to touch me, but she didn't. The hand slid into the pocket of her jeans. "I'll be right back," she said.

I sat on the edge of my chair, pried the lid off my cup and blew on the hot chocolate.

"Are you really all right?" Rafe asked.

"Yeah," I said automatically. I looked over at Anne, standing at the triage desk. "No," I said, and then I turned back to Rafe. "But I'm getting there."

33

I fell asleep with my head on Rafe's shoulder and the arm of the chair jammed against my ribs. I woke to the sound of my dad's voice, low and quiet, talking to Anne.

I sat up. My mouth tasted sour and sticky.

"I'm sorry," Dad said. He leaned across Anne. "I was trying not to wake you."

"It's okay," I mumbled, pushing at my hair. "How's Jason?"

"All right. He's awake. They're getting ready to take him up to a room."

I let out the breath I hadn't realized I was holding. The waiting room whirled around me. I grabbed the chair arm and squeezed my eyes shut for a moment.

"Take a deep breath," Rafe whispered.

I reached for his hand and opened my eyes. "Can I see him?" I asked.

"After he's settled," Dad said. His eyes were bloodshot and he needed a shave. "I'll come get you." He gestured in the direction of the triage desk. "I have to get back to Jason."

"We'll be right here," Anne said.

Dad shot me a quick glance before he started back. I thought he was going to say something else, but he didn't.

It was close to an hour before we got to see Jason.

The second week of school my history class had spent the afternoon at the Highland Games. Propped up in bed, Jason was the same color as the haggis (which I'd discovered was sheep organs and oatmeal boiled in the sheep's stomach). The scrapes on his cheek glistened with yellow ointment. They looked worse with all the gravel cleaned away.

I moved over beside the bed. Behind me, Dad leaned against the doorframe as if he was too tired to stand up by himself. Anne had a hand on his arm as though she was helping keep him upright. I'd persuaded Rafe to go home.

"Hey, you're here," Jason croaked. He stopped to swallow and grimaced. "I figured you'd be so pissed off you'd..." another swallow, "...go home." He pushed himself up a little higher and sucked in a sharp breath as he moved his right arm. "Izzy, I'm sorry. Won't happen again—"

"—swear to God it won't," I said, cutting him off before he said the words. I knew the speech by heart. I'd heard it enough times.

A rushing, drumming sound, like water beating on my head, filled my ears. I moved to the side of the bed. Jason wasn't different, but this time I was. "You just had a little too much, right?" I said. "A little too much to drink, a little too many pills. What's the difference?"

"I had some drinks," Jason said. His eyes kept sliding off my face as though they couldn't stay focused. "Sorry."

How many times had Jason said that? When you say a word over and over and over again, eventually it stops meaning anything. Just the way "sorry" did when it was coming out of Jason's mouth.

I heard Dad move behind me. "Shut up," I said, working to keep my voice steady.

Jason sighed and closed his eyes for a second. "Iz," he started.

I didn't let him finish. "Shut up." I said it louder this time and then I leaned over the bed and shoved him back against the pillow. He made a garbled sound full of pain and shock. I hit him on the side of the head.

He clenched his teeth and moaned. His lips were blue.

Dad grabbed both my arms. "Jesus, Isabelle. What's the matter with you?" he shouted.

Jason had rolled half onto his side. He clutched his right arm and tried to get his breath.

Dad twisted me around to face him. "Wait in the hallway," he said. A tiny tic twitched at the corner of his left eye.

I wrenched out of his grip. My hands were clenched into fists so tightly it looked like the knuckles would pop through the skin.

Anne stuck an arm between us. "Marc, let her finish," she said.

Dad looked at her as if she'd suggested we throw Jason out the window. "Christ, Anne. He just had his stomach pumped."

Anne looked at me. Her eyes flicked over to Jason for a second. "No more hitting," she said.

I gave a slight nod and my breath came out in ragged bursts like I'd been running.

Anne took hold of both Dad's arms, the same way he'd been holding me. "Let Isabelle say what she needs to say." She looked up at him and he couldn't seem to look away. "Please."

"Say whatever you have to say," he said after a long moment, his eyes never leaving Anne's face. "And do it quickly."

I turned back to Jason.

"I don't know…what your problem is," he said, the words coming out in a raspy whisper. "You wanna beat on me? Later. I'm tired." He slumped against the pillow and closed his eyes.

"Oh, boo-hoo," I said. Jason's eyes came open again.

His leather jacket lay across the arm of a blue vinyl chair that was pulled up next to the bed. We'd found it underneath him when the paramedics lifted him onto the stretcher. I grabbed it and hugged it to my chest. The jacket smelled like beer and puke. "This is mine, Jason," I said, my voice shaking. "Consider it a down payment on all the money you bummed from me to get wrecked."

"Don't start," Jason wheezed.

"You're a filthy, stinking, gross drunk," I continued as though he had never said a word. "You're a lousy brother and a lousy human being. You're a piece of crap, Jason." I had to shove my hands into my pockets because I really did think I might hit him again.

"Isabelle, you need to go home," I heard my father's exhausted voice say behind me.

"Let her…" another ragged swallow "…Dad." Jason had that cocky look he got whenever he thought he'd pulled one over on someone. I couldn't make him stop. I couldn't make him change. He didn't care how I felt. Or Dad. Or Anne.

I thought my legs would buckle. I put one hand out behind me and found the wall. "I thought you were dead," I whispered. "When I came around the side of the fountain and saw you, I thought you were dead this time. And I didn't want to touch you because I knew the moment I did it would be true." My voice cracked. I felt Anne's hands on my shoulders. She was almost holding me up, my legs were shaking so badly now.

"But you weren't dead. Not this time. So will it be the next time? Or the one after that?"

Jason turned away from me and stared out the window.

"I can't give you any more chances, Jason," I said. "And I can't love you anymore." My eyes filled with tears.

I pulled away from Anne and ran out into the hallway. The green tile floor shimmered under my feet. Tears dripped off my chin onto Jason's jacket.

Anne came out of the room. Tears were sliding down her own face. She reached over and wiped my cheek with the heel of her hand. "Let's go home," she said.

She put both arms around me and I sagged against her. And I didn't pull away.

34

We didn't talk on the way home. Anne paid the taxi driver and we climbed the front steps and went into the house, still without saying a word. I took off my sweatshirt and draped it over the bottom stair post. I didn't know what to do. All the tears were cried out and all my fury was gone. I was empty.

Anne hung up her jacket and wiped her palms on her jeans. "Would you like something to eat?" she asked.

I shook my head. "Thanks, but I just want to get out of these clothes and have a shower."

She studied my face for a moment, her lower lip caught between her teeth. "Okay," she said. "I'm here if you need anything."

I felt awkward, weird, as though coming home had changed everything back to the way it used to be between us.

Anne disappeared in the direction of the kitchen and I started up the stairs. Halfway up I stopped. A déjà vu, goose-bumps-up-my-back feeling came over me. How many times had I done this to Anne since the wedding? Even before then it had always been "No, thanks" and off to my room.

I sat on a step and leaned my head against the banister railing. I couldn't figure out how I felt about Anne now. Guilty, that was for sure. Because of the baby. Because Anne had always been nice to me and most of the time I'd been a brat.

I thought about all the mornings I'd sat at the table and pretty much ignored her. I thought about her telling Dad that she was going to look for Jason. I remembered her face, the way it glowed when she showed me the sonogram, and I remembered the way she'd looked the day she'd come home from the hospital with no baby.

I was ashamed of myself. There was a lot about Anne that I didn't know and I realized that I wanted to.

Anne was chopping mushrooms at the kitchen counter, a red-and-white-checked dishtowel tucked in the waist of her pants. I hesitated in the doorway. "Um, Anne?"

She looked over her shoulder at me.

"I, uh, I guess I am sort of hungry," I said. "What can I do?"

She smiled, a small smile but a real one. "You could grate some mozzarella."

"Okay." I rummaged in the fridge for the cheese and found the grater in the cupboard next to the dishwasher. We worked without talking for a few minutes.

Anne finished the mushrooms and crossed behind me to get the eggs. I'd shredded a little mountain of cheese onto a plate. "That looks like enough," she said.

She beat the eggs with a fork and heated a little butter in a pan. I leaned on the counter and watched. When the omelet was done and cut in half, we sat across from each other at the table and ate.

Spencer wandered in, whiskers twitching. I lifted him onto my lap and fed him a cheesy bit of egg. He gobbled it down and looked expectantly at me. When I took the next bite for myself he put a paw on my hand.

"Can you teach me how to do this?" I asked, with my mouth full of fluffy egg, gooey cheese, mushrooms and some kind of herb I couldn't identify.

"Sure," Anne said. "It's not that hard. Will you teach me how to make your spaghetti sauce?"

"Yeah, next time I make it." I gave Spencer another taste, then took one myself and chased it with a big bite of the crusty bread Anne had toasted under the broiler. "The secret to the sauce is the meatballs. I don't use hamburger."

Anne's fork stopped halfway to her mouth. "Aww, please tell me they're not tofu." She smushed up her mouth when she said "tofu."

"No, they're not tofu," I said. "But what's wrong with it?"

"It looks like white play clay." She shuddered.

"So? It doesn't taste like play clay."

"You've tasted play clay?"

"I ate half a can of the fluorescent pink stuff the third day of kindergarten."

"Why?"

I held up both hands and shrugged. "How else could I find out what it tasted like?"

Anne burst out laughing. "Yeah, but half a can?"

"I was trying to decide whether I liked the taste."

"So did you?"

"Nah. It was like eating an eraser."

"So's tofu," Anne said, pointing at me as if she'd just scored a point.

I couldn't help laughing too. I liked the way it felt.

I fed Spencer his own food and gave him some milk. Anne and I did the dishes at the sink instead of loading them into the dishwasher. We were almost finished when Dad came in. I could see the tracks of his fingers through his hair. There was stubble on his cheeks and dark circles, like purple bruises, under his eyes.

"How's Jason?" Anne asked, grabbing a piece of paper towel to wipe her hands.

Dad closed his eyes for a second and my throat suddenly began to ache. I knew what was coming. He sat at the table and Anne got him a cup of coffee.

Jason didn't think he had a drinking problem. Jason wouldn't get help because he didn't need help.

"I don't know what to do," Dad said, rubbing his face.

Anne put her hand on his shoulder for a moment and then slid it down his arm and took hold of his hand. I leaned, silent, against the sink. Anne looked over at me.

No way, I thought. Because even though she wasn't saying anything out loud, it was as though I could hear her asking me to come over to my father. Yeah. Then what? Hug and have a Hallmark moment? I stared at my feet but I could still feel Anne looking at me.

I was too tired to think straight—or even crooked for that matter. Jason. Dad. I had a totally screwed-up family.

And then I remembered Mrs. Mac telling me what her mother had said about families, the day Jason had shown up at the Seniors Center to borrow money from me: When family needs taking care of, you have to do it, even if you don't want to.

Right.

I didn't want to. But we were a family. Not what I'd wanted, that's for sure, but …

I looked up. Anne's eyes were still on me. Dad's were closed. His face was gray, the lines all going down.

Mrs. Mac was close to eighty. Which would have made her mother at least a hundred if she hadn't been dead. I was taking advice from a hundred-year-old dead person.

But I did it. I went over to Dad, put my arms around his neck and hugged him. It was clumsy, like I had half a dozen arms instead of two. "It's okay, Dad," I said. "We'll figure something out."

His free arm came around my waist and he hugged me tightly against him. It was a heart-tugging movie-of-the-week moment. But it felt okay.

35

i was lying on the bed, my wet hair hanging over the side, too wired to sleep, when someone tapped on my door.

"Come in," I said, arching my neck back as far as it could go so I could see who was there.

Dad stood in the doorway. "Got a minute?" he asked.

"Uh, yeah, sure." I rolled over and sat up.

"I wanted to tell you…" He trailed off. His hands were jammed into the pockets of his khakis, but I could see them flexing and clenching.

He began again. "Anne and I have decided how we're going to handle things with Jason. And, uh, I wanted to tell you."

"Okay." I pulled my hair down over one shoulder and combed slowly through it with my fingers.

"I can't just give up on Jason," Dad said. "I was wrong about that. But I can't pretend he's not a drunk and a drug addict."

"So what do we do?"

He stared past me out the window for a moment. "He'll have food and somewhere to sleep but that's it." The lines around his mouth deepened and he winced as he said the words, like it was painful letting them out.

"I'm not giving Jason any money or anything that he can sell for money. And when he's here, in this house, no drugs, no alcohol."

"It sounds like a plan."

"I need your promise that you won't give him any money either."

"I won't. I swear."

"I don't know if it's the right way to do this," Dad said, looking at me again. "But this is how we're going to handle things for now."

To my horror my eyes began to sting. All I could do was nod.

He cleared his throat and swallowed. I wondered what was coming next. "You were right," he said slowly. "I've been a lousy father. If I could go back and be better, I would."

A squirmy feeling came over me. I didn't want him to say it. It didn't seem so important to be right anymore. "You weren't that bad," I said.

"I wasn't that good, either." He closed his eyes for a second, shook his head. "I won't tell you I'm going to turn into Superdad. I will do better, but I don't know how much better that will be."

"I, uh, was a brat sometimes too," I said.

Dad smiled. "True. But you're a teenager. It's part of your job description."

I gave him a small smile back and swallowed down the lump that had suddenly appeared in my throat.

"Get some rest," Dad said. "Anne and I are going out to eat later. Why don't you come with us?"

I started to say no automatically and caught myself. "Um, yeah," I said instead.

"I'll give you a yell in a little while," he said and then he was gone.

I flopped back on the bed and pressed my hands over my eyes. My eyelids felt like two little inflatable pillows. I was exhausted, but I wasn't sleepy.

I let my arms drop onto the bed. Long fingers of light stretched across the ceiling from the window. My mom's picture smiled at me from the dresser. What rule would she have for this, I wondered, for dealing with Jason and this whole deeply weird family?

Maybe there weren't rules for everything. Maybe sometimes you had to wing it. Rafe had told me that more than once. Maybe he was right. Not that I was going to tell him that.

I closed my eyes. Thinking was making my brain hurt.

After a bit I rolled off the bed and went over to the dresser. The little red notebook with all the rules was lying next to my mother's picture. I picked up the book and opened the bottom dresser drawer. The ultrasound picture was still there. I stared at it for a long moment. Then I turned the picture face up, set the notebook next to it and closed the drawer. If I ever needed to look at either one again, they'd be easy to find.

Jason didn't show up for four days. When he walked in, shaved, wearing clean jeans and smelling like spearmint gum, Dad told him what they had decided—what we had decided.

Dad stood by the kitchen table. Anne was in the doorway, arms crossed. I leaned against the counter, hands in my pockets. But the three of us could just as easily have been side by side, arms linked, singing "Blowin' in the Wind" or some other old-time song of solidarity.

"We love you, Jason," Dad said. "Me, Anne, your sister, we're right here for you. If you want to be here with us, you have to do it straight and sober."

Jason did all his routines. He joked; he made excuses. He was wounded and offended and finally he got mad and left, the door yawning open behind him.

36

I'm not sure whose idea the cooking lesson was. Mrs. Mac showed up at the door one day with a pan of cinnamon rolls—probably the best thing I had ever tasted in my life—and Anne was there and they started talking and then Lisa came and she joined in and somehow everyone ended up in our kitchen on a wet Saturday afternoon making cinnamon rolls.

"I didn't know you even liked to cook," I said to Lisa.

She shrugged. "I figure between the munchkins at Dad's and my mom going macrobiotic, it's the only way I'm ever going to get anything to eat other than Zoodles and organic stir-fried bean curd."

The whole process was too complicated for me. I'd rather go down to Rye's for a blueberry muffin and a cup of hot chocolate, sit in the window and watch the little piece of stubble on the left side of Rafe's chin that he always missed when he shaved.

So I greased pans, washed dishes and swept at least two cups of flour off the kitchen floor. Spencer went from person to person, getting his chin scratched. His purr sounded like a car with a bad muffler. Dad refused to even step inside the kitchen. "Call me when there's something edible," he said. Then he grinned. "If there is." Anne threw an oven mitt at him.

Rafe, on the other hand, hung around the kitchen like a dog waiting for someone to throw him a scrap from the table. Finally Anne sent him out to the gourmet coffee place for a pound of some kind of coffee I'd never heard of.

Anne and Lisa crouched in front of the oven door, gleefully watching the rolls bake and grinning like a couple of five year olds at a magic show.

Mrs. Mac was beating icing sugar and milk in a small metal bowl at the counter. I draped an arm around her and lay my head on her shoulder for a second. "Thank you," I said.

She reached up and touched my cheek. "You're welcome, dear," she said. "I like your family and your friends."

I gave her a squeeze. "Me too."

It was still raining. I stood in the front window and watched raindrops splash into the puddles. And then I looked up the street toward the corner. I couldn't help it. At least three or four times a day since Jason had taken off, I found myself at the window hoping somehow I'd see him coming up the sidewalk.

As I stood there, someone turned the corner. He—or she—wore an old, too-big green slicker. Water dripped off the hood. For maybe the hundredth time since the night he'd stormed off, I wished it were Jason.

And then, as the person got closer, I saw that it was.

Darlene Ryan has been a swimming instructor, a copywriter and a late-night disc jockey. Now a full-time writer, she counts Robert Munsch as one of her heroes and tries to live by the immortal words of Ms. Frizzell from the Magic School Bus: "Take chances, make mistakes, get messy."

Darlene wrote *Rules for Life*, her first teen novel, because, in her own words, "Families fascinate me. They are the people we're supposed to love the most and we often end up treating them the worst. This book began, like almost all my writing does, with What if? What if you could talk to your dad about absolutely anything? What if your brother was the world's biggest screwup? What would that make you?"

Darlene is also the author of *A Mother's Adoption Journey* (Second Story Press), based on her experiences adopting a daughter from China, and *Kisses, Kisses, Kisses* from the University of New Brunswick. She lives in Fredericton, New Brunswick.

Other Recent Fiction
from Orca Book Publishers

Available at bookstores
or directly from Orca
800-210-5277
www.orcabook.com